WALKING by FAITH

Two / Jesus Christ

Principal Program Consultants

Rev. Terry M. Odien, MA

Rev. Michael D. Place, STD

Dr. Addie Lorraine Walker, SSND

Harcourt
Religion Publishers

Nihil Obstat
Rev. Dwayne J. Thoman
Censor Deputatus

Imprimatur
✠ Most Rev. Jerome Hanus, OSB
Archbishop of Dubuque
September 17, 1997
Feast of Saint Robert Bellarmine, Patron of Catechists

The Ad Hoc Committee to Oversee the Use of the Catechism, National Conference of Catholic Bishops, has found this catechetical series to be in conformity with the *Catechism of the Catholic Church.*

For permission to reprint copyrighted material, grateful acknowledgment is made to the following sources:

American Bible Society: Scripture selections from *THE HOLY BIBLE: Contemporary English Version.* Text copyright © 1995 by American Bible Society.

Confraternity of Christian Doctrine, Washington, D.C.: Scripture selections from *NEW AMERICAN BIBLE.* Text copyright © 1991, 1986, 1970 by the Confraternity of Christian Doctrine. Used by license of the copyright owner. All rights reserved. No part of *NEW AMERICAN BIBLE* may be reproduced, by any means, without permission in writing from the copyright holder.

English Language Liturgical Consultation (ELLC): English translation of the "Lord's Prayer." Text © 1988 by the English Language Liturgical Consultation.

International Committee on English in the Liturgy, Inc. (ICEL): From the English translation of *Rite of Baptism for Children.* Text © 1969 by ICEL. From the English translation of *The Roman Missal.* Text © 1973 by ICEL. From the English translation of *Rite of Penance.* Text © 1974 by ICEL. From the English translation of *Rite of Confirmation,* Second Edition. Text © 1975 by ICEL. From the English translations of *A Book of Prayers* and *Pastoral Care of the Sick: Rites of Anointing and Viaticum.* Text © 1982 by ICEL. From the English translation of *Rite of Christian Initiation of Adults.* Text © 1985 by ICEL. From the English translation of *Book of Blessings.* Text © 1988 by ICEL. All rights reserved.

Cover illustration by Bill James

A Blessing for Beginnings

"So we are always courageous . . .
for we walk by faith. . . ."

—2 Corinthians 5:6–7

Leader: This year we come together to continue our journey of faith. We are ready to learn from one another and from our Church community. And so we pray: God our Father, you sent your Son, Jesus Christ, as a gift to the world. Through him we learn more about you and how you want us to live. Be with us on our journey to you, and fill us with your grace.

Reader: Listen to God's message to us: (*Read Isaiah 11:1–9.*) The word of the Lord.

All: Thanks be to God.

Leader: Let us ask God's blessing on our journey this year.

All: God—Father, Son, and Holy Spirit— walk with us. Help us listen to your message and live by Jesus' example. Keep us always in the grace of your friendship. We ask this in faith, as brothers and sisters of Jesus.

Leader: May the Lord be with us, now and always.

All: Amen!

WALKING by FAITH

Two / Jesus Christ

A Blessing for Beginnings 3

Unit One   **God's Gift to Our World**
Chapter 1   Beginnings 6
Chapter 2   A World of Signs 12
Chapter 3   God's Promise Is Forever 18
Unit One Checkpoint 24
Chapter 4   We Celebrate Mary: Saying Yes to God 26

Unit Two   **Jesus Teaches Us About God**
Chapter 5   The Father of Jesus 30
Chapter 6   God Gives Us Life 36
Chapter 7   The Holy Spirit Is with Us 42
Unit Two Checkpoint 48
Chapter 8   We Celebrate All Saints: Stars for God 50

Unit Three   **Jesus Shares Himself with Us**
Chapter 9   Jesus Shows Us How to Love 54
Chapter 10   Jesus Feeds Us 60
Chapter 11   Jesus Forgives Us 66
Unit Three Checkpoint 72
Chapter 12   We Celebrate Advent: Come, Lord Jesus! 74

Unit Four   **Jesus Lives in the Church**

Chapter 13   The Church Is a Community 78
Chapter 14   Doing the Work of Jesus 84
Chapter 15   The Church Remembers Jesus 90
Unit Four Checkpoint 96

Chapter 16   *We Celebrate Christmas: Jesus Is Born* 98

Unit Five   **The Sacrament of Reconciliation**

Chapter 17   Jesus Invites Us to Love 102
Chapter 18   We Make Choices 108
Chapter 19   We Celebrate Forgiveness 114
Unit Five Checkpoint 120

Chapter 20   *We Celebrate Lent: A Time of Sacrifice* 122

Unit Six   **Jesus Gives Us Sacraments**

Chapter 21   The Church Welcomes Us 126
Chapter 22   Jesus Is with Us 132
Chapter 23   Members of the Church 138
Unit Six Checkpoint 144

Chapter 24   *We Celebrate Holy Week: Good Friday* 146

Unit Seven   **Jesus, Lord of All Creation**

Chapter 25   God Invites Us 150
Chapter 26   Jesus Will Come Again 156
Chapter 27   We Care for the World 162
Unit Seven Checkpoint 168

Chapter 28   *We Celebrate Easter: New Life in Jesus* 170

Catholic Prayers and Resources 174
The Language of Faith 183
Index 191

CHAPTER 1

Beginnings

PRAYER

Thank you, God our Father, for sending us Jesus! Help us learn to know you better this year, as we learn about your Son.

Mark woke up before it was light. He couldn't wait for this day to start. Today Mark's mom was coming home with his new baby sister, Sara.

Mark looked out the window. Everything seemed to have changed. The same old street looked new. Even Mark felt different. Now he was a big brother. He had a whole new person to get to know and love.

Mark heard his dad let the dog out. Dad was up early, too. Mark smiled. Today was a new beginning.

- **How do you feel when you are starting something new?**

ACTIVITY

Today is a new beginning for us, too. Tell one thing you want to learn about in religion class this year.

This picture shows how one artist painted Jesus' birth. How do you think Mary and Joseph felt when Jesus was born?

A Special Baby

Every new baby is a new beginning. Long ago in a little town called *Bethlehem*, a very special baby was born. This baby's birth was a new beginning for the whole world.

The baby's mother was named Mary. Her husband was a kind, strong man named Joseph. They named the baby Jesus.

Jesus was human like us. He needed a family to care for him, just as every baby does. But Jesus was also the **Son of God**. God sent Jesus into our world. Jesus brought God's great love to us in a special way so we could see it and feel it.

Catholics Believe . . .

that Jesus is both God and human. He is Mary's child and the Son of God.

Catechism, #423

We learn to follow Jesus in our everyday lives. We practice loving and caring at home and in school.

Catechism, #533

How can you show that you care for your family?

Just Like Us

Even though Jesus was the Son of God, he grew up just like us. He learned to walk and talk and pray. He played games and sang songs. He helped Mary carry water from the town well and bake bread in an outdoor oven. He helped Joseph in the family carpenter shop. They made useful and beautiful things from wood.

We call Jesus, Mary, and Joseph the **Holy Family**. The word *holy* means "like God." Jesus' family was holy because they always did their best to show God's love and care. Their life was not always easy. They did not have much money. They lived in a country that was ruled by a powerful army. But through all times the Holy Family trusted God.

The Holy Family was like all families. They shared the same troubles and joys.

Mary and Joseph taught Jesus about God, his Father. They told Jesus stories about God's love and answered Jesus' questions. Here is one story they told.

SCRIPTURE STORY

Our World Begins

In the beginning there was no world. There was only God. And there was a big empty place. God's loving Spirit breathed on the emptiness. And God said, "Let there be light!"

There was light. God created light. And one by one, day by day, God created more things. God created sun and moon, mountains and rivers, sky and sea. God made everything there is. Stars twinkled. Trees grew from tiny seeds. Birds flew. Giant animals and tiny fish jumped for joy. Last and best of all, God made people. And God said, "This is very good!"

We were made by God to be God-like. What a great beginning!

—based on Genesis 1:1–2:4

RECALL

Who is the Son of God? Who are the members of the Holy Family?

THINK AND SHARE

Why do you think people tell the story about how our world began?

CONTINUE THE JOURNEY

Jesus helped his family. Draw a picture of yourself helping your family.

WE LIVE OUR FAITH

At Home Ask an older family member to tell about the day you first came home to join your family. Or tell a younger brother or sister how you felt when he or she was born.

In the Parish Look for pictures or statues of the Holy Family in your church or classroom. Pray for all the families in your parish.

A Good Start

Like Jesus, we start our lives in families. Our families can teach us about God and share God's love with us. Praying for our families is a good way to say thank you to God.

Pray these words together. Think about your family as you pray.

PRAYER

Dear God, you made us.
You call us to grow in love,
and you sent your Son, Jesus, to
   show us how.
Thank you for giving us people to
   care for us,
as Joseph and Mary cared for Jesus.
Help our families be holy
   families, too.

CHAPTER 2

A World of Signs

PRAYER

Dear God, we thank you for the world you made. Help us see signs of your love everywhere.

How can you tell that someone loves you? You can use your eyes, your ears, your hands, and even your nose!

Rachel smells stew cooking. Stew is her favorite dinner. She knows her father is making stew as a sign of love for his family.

Tim feels the soft, woolly sweater his aunt knitted. The sweater keeps him warm like a hug.

Rosa hears someone call her name. She sees her best friend, Luisa, running across the playground. Rosa can hardly wait to eat lunch with her friend.

ACTIVITY

Name a sign of love that you have seen, heard, or touched.

Jesus Saw Signs of Love

Jesus found many signs of love in the world around him. When he was growing up in the town of *Nazareth*, Jesus learned about love from his family. He tasted love in the fresh bread Mary baked. He touched love in the wooden bench Joseph made for him.

Most of all, Jesus saw signs of God's love. The world God made is full of signs.

Jesus watched the birds flying in the high, blue sky. He saw them come home to their nests in the rocky hillsides. Jesus watched wildflowers cover the desert with gold after a rainstorm. He saw how a tiny mustard seed grew into a huge plant.

"Look!" Jesus wanted to shout to everyone. "See how much God cares for us!"

ACTIVITY

Signs of God's love are everywhere. Draw your favorite thing that God made.

Saints Walk with Us
Hildegard of Bingen

Hildegard saw God's love everywhere in the world. She wrote songs and plays and painted pictures praising God.

This is one of Hildegard's paintings. How would you draw a picture of God's love?

Stories and Signs

When Jesus grew up, he began to travel around his country. He told people about God's love. He invited people to look for signs of God's love in **creation**, the world God made.

Jesus remembered the stories that Mary had told him. He told stories, too. These stories were about flocks of sheep and fields of grain and loaves of bread rising in the oven. The stories were about things people could see all around them. Jesus' stories helped people see God's love in their lives.

Jesus shared God's love in other ways, too. He healed sick people. He fed hungry people. He made those who were left out feel welcome. In all his actions Jesus used signs of creation, like water and bread and sweet-smelling oil. He helped people look at creation in a new way.

The Book of God's Love

We still tell and read the same stories Jesus heard. We remember the stories that Jesus told people. All these stories of God's love are found in the **Bible**, our holy book. The word *Bible* means "a collection of books." Even though a Bible looks like only one book, it is really many books put together.

The word **Scripture** means "holy writing." *Scripture* is another word for the Bible.

ACTIVITY

As a class, decorate the table where your Bible is displayed.

Stepping Stones

Getting to Know the Bible

Here are some things you can do to get to know the Bible better:

• Look at a Bible at home or in school. See how many books are in the Bible.

• Listen carefully to the readings from Scripture at Mass.

• The library has many Bible storybooks with pictures. Read a Bible story on your own or with your family. Then tell the story to someone else.

Where Will This Lead Me?

Getting to know the Bible is one way to get to know Jesus. Reading or listening to the stories of the Bible is like hearing God speak to you.

RECALL

When did Jesus use the signs of creation to tell people about God's love? What is the Bible?

THINK AND SHARE

What are some ways we use the signs of creation in church?

CONTINUE THE JOURNEY

Make up a story about an ordinary thing or activity that shows God's love. Draw a picture to go with your story.

WE LIVE OUR FAITH

At Home Go on a walk with a family member. Together, make a list of five signs of God's love you see in your neighborhood.

In the Parish Listen carefully to the Scripture readings at Mass. If you have any questions about what you hear, ask the priest, a family member, or your teacher.

Praise God!

The Bible says that all creation sings to God (*Isaiah 6:3*). We join in that song at Mass. We praise God in words and music.

Read the prayer below. Think about what each line of the prayer means. The word *hosanna* means "Praise God!" in Hebrew. Hebrew is one of the languages Jesus used when he prayed.

Praise God together by reading or singing the words in bold print.

PRAYER

Holy, holy, holy Lord, God of power and might,
(No one is as great as God! God can do anything!)

heaven and earth are full of your glory.
(Signs of God's love are everywhere in creation.)

Hosanna in the highest.

Blessed is he who comes in the name of the Lord.
(We are glad that Jesus came to show us God's love!)

Hosanna in the highest.

CHAPTER 3

God's Promise Is Forever

PRAYER

God our Father, you promised to love us forever. Thank you for keeping your promise by sending Jesus!

Amanda wore her new necklace to Laura's party. She took the necklace off to play games and forgot about it.

Laura's mother found the necklace. "Promise me you'll take this to Amanda tomorrow," Laura's mother said.

"I promise," Laura said. But the more Laura looked at the necklace, the more she liked it. "This is pretty," Laura thought. "Nobody gave me a pretty necklace for my birthday. Maybe I'll just keep it for myself."

- **What does it mean to make a promise? Why is it important to keep a promise?**

What would you tell Laura to do? Why?

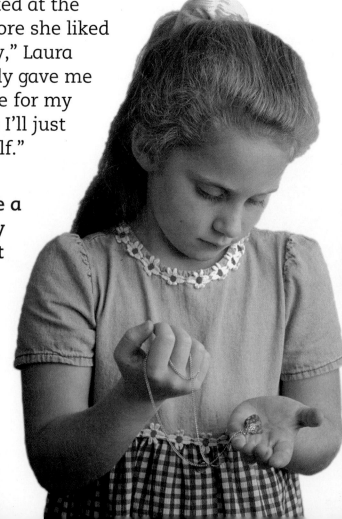

God did not make bad things like war, pollution, and violence. These things are caused by people choosing to sin.

A Broken Promise

God has loved us from the very beginning. God promised to love and trust the first people forever. The first people promised that they would always love and trust God, too.

The Bible tells us that the first people broke their promise. They turned away from God's love. They stopped trusting in God. They made the choice to **sin**, or break away from God's friendship.

Broken promises hurt people. All God's creation was hurt by the first people's broken promise. Sadness came into God's good and happy world.

The first people chose not to be friends with God. But they could not lose God's love because that love has no end. God promised to send someone who would show people the way back to his friendship. God kept that promise by sending Jesus, his own Son. In Jesus God became one of us so that we could become like God.

Catholics Believe . . .

that God loves us always. God sent Jesus to bring all people back into God's friendship.

Catechism, #457

The Good Shepherd

Scripture Signpost

"God loved the people of this world so much that he gave his only Son. . . ."

John 3:16

Jesus once told his friends a story about love and promises. He told them about a shepherd who promised to take care of some sheep. The shepherd loved the sheep. He knew each one of them by name. The sheep knew the shepherd's voice. They knew they were safe when the shepherd was with them.

Every night the shepherd would lead the sheep into a pen. The pen had only one opening. The shepherd would lie down with his body across the opening. That way, if a wolf came to attack the sheep, it would run into the shepherd first. The shepherd knew he might die if a wolf attacked him. But he had promised to care for his sheep. He would give his life for them.

—*based on John 10:1–18*

Jesus Saves Us

Jesus was like the shepherd in the story. He came to show us that sin, sadness, and death will not win. God's love is the only thing that will last forever.

Everything Jesus said and did was meant to remind us of God's promise. Jesus' whole life was like a map showing us how to return to God's friendship. Jesus gave away his whole life so that we could be saved. He died on the cross for us. Jesus trusted God's promise completely. So God gave Jesus new life.

The name *Jesus* means "God saves us." The chart below shows some other names we use for Jesus and what they mean.

Landmark The *crucifix* shows Jesus on the cross. It is a reminder that Jesus gave his life for us. You will often see a crucifix near the altar in church.

Names for Jesus

Savior
- "the one who saves us"

Lord
- a name for God. Jesus' friends called him *Lord* as a sign of respect. They also called him *Teacher*.

Christ
- "God's chosen one, anointed with oil." People in Jesus' time used sweet-smelling oil as a sign of specialness.

Messiah
- the same as Christ, but in the Hebrew language

RECALL
What is sin? Why do we call Jesus our Savior?

THINK AND SHARE
Why do you think people sometimes break promises?

CONTINUE THE JOURNEY
Fill out the promise sheet. Color the seal.

I, _____,
(YOUR NAME)

promise to love and trust

God forever. I will keep my

promise by _____

_____.
(ONE WAY YOU WILL SHOW THAT YOU LOVE GOD)

WE LIVE OUR FAITH

At Home   Make a promise to help someone in your family. Tell him or her about it, and keep your promise!

In the Parish   Make the Sign of the Cross with holy water when you enter or leave the church. This is a sign of the promise you (or your family) made at Baptism to always love and trust God. The cross is also the sign that God promises us new life with Jesus.

Have Mercy

All people sin. Only Jesus and Mary, his mother, loved and trusted God so much that they never chose to turn away from God's love. But Jesus came to tell us that God will forgive us if we are sorry. God will show loving kindness even when we have broken our promises.

Wherever Jesus went, he reminded people of God's love. Sinners came to Jesus to ask for *mercy*. We can pray in words like theirs *(Luke 18:38)*. These words are called the *Jesus Prayer*.

PRAYER

Lord Jesus Christ,
Son of the living God,
have mercy on me, a sinner!

Review

Fill in the Blanks
Complete each sentence with the correct term from the word bank.

1. We call Jesus, Mary, and Joseph the _____ Family.

2. The _____ is our holy book.

3. The first people chose to _____, or turn away from God's friendship.

4. God shows _____ to people who are sorry for sin.

5. A crucifix shows Jesus on the _____.

Word Bank

Bible   cross   Holy   forgiveness   sin

Who Am I?
Match each description in Column A with the correct name from Column B.

Column A

_____ 1. I wrote songs and painted pictures of creation.

_____ 2. My name means "God saves us."

_____ 3. I took care of Mary and Jesus.

_____ 4. I am the mother of Jesus.

_____ 5. I take care of the sheep.

Column B

a. Joseph

b. Hildegard

c. Mary

d. Jesus

e. the Good Shepherd

Share Your Faith
Imagine you meet someone who has never heard of Jesus. Tell that person what you know about Jesus. Why is he so important?

Show How Far You've Come

Use the chart below to show what you have learned. For each chapter, draw or write one important thing you remember.

God's Gift to Our World

Chapter 1 Beginnings	Chapter 2 A World of Signs	Chapter 3 God's Promise Is Forever

What Else Would You Like to Know?

List any questions you still have about Jesus and God's creation.

_____

_____

Continue the Journey

Choose one or more of the following activities to do on your own, with your class, or with your family.

- Look through your Faith Journal pages for Unit One. Choose your favorite activity, and share it with a friend or family member.

- Choose a favorite Bible story about Jesus or a story Jesus told. Act out the story, or make your own storybook with pictures.

- Do something to care for God's creation. Plant a garden, take care of an animal, or recycle old newspapers. Tell how your project is a way of serving God.

Saying Yes to God

PRAYER

Mother Mary, God the Father chose you to love and care for Jesus. Help us say yes to God as you did.

What do you do when you have to make an important choice? God asked Mary, Jesus' mother, to make the most important choice of all.

SCRIPTURE STORY
Mary's Answer

God sent the Angel Gabriel to Mary. **Angels** are spirits who serve God and bring God's message to people.

Gabriel greeted Mary. "God has chosen you," Gabriel said. "God wants you to be the mother of Jesus, who will save all people."

Mary loved and trusted God very much. She knew God would not ask her to do something impossible. So she answered, "Yes! I will do what God wants."

—based on Luke 1:26–38

Most of the time, messages from God don't come through angels. How do we know what God wants us to do?

Blessed Are You

God did not force Mary to be Jesus' mother. He gave Mary a choice, and she said yes. God gives each of us a choice, too. Every day he asks for our love and our trust. We can say yes in everything we do.

Mary will help us say yes to God. Jesus' mother is a mother to us. She cares for us. She shows us how to trust in God. We can ask her to pray for us.

The Hail Mary is our special prayer to Mary. The chart tells what the words of this prayer mean.

Catholics Believe . . .

that Mary, the mother of Jesus, shows us how to love and trust God.

Catechism, #494

Our Prayer to Mary

Words of the Prayer	What the Words Mean
Hail, Mary, full of grace.	Be joyful, Mary! You are full of God's life and love.
The Lord is with you.	God is very close to you.
Blessed are you among women,	God has chosen you out of all people.
and blessed is the fruit of your womb, Jesus.	The baby who grows inside you is holy.
Holy Mary, Mother of God,	Mary, you obey God in all things. You are the mother of Jesus, who is God.
pray for us sinners	We ask you to bring our prayers to God. We ask for God's mercy.
now and at the hour of our death.	Be with us every moment of our lives.
Amen.	Yes, we believe this!

RECALL

Who brought God's message to Mary? What is the name of our special prayer to Mary?

THINK AND SHARE

Why do you think Mary said yes to God?

CONTINUE THE JOURNEY

Draw a picture of Mary saying yes to God.

Y
E
S!

A
M
E
N!

WE LIVE OUR FAITH

 At Home Ask family members to help you learn how to make good choices.

In the Parish As a class, be "angels" for a needy family with a new baby. Write a letter to the new baby. Welcome him or her into the world. Collect extra baby clothes and toys for the family.

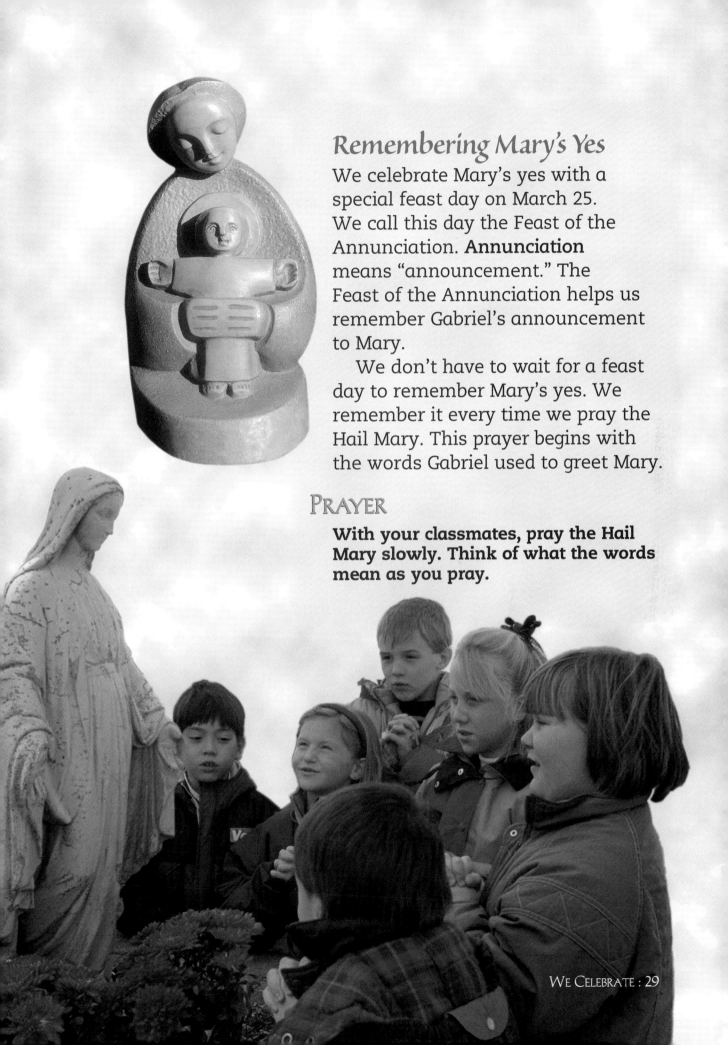

Remembering Mary's Yes

We celebrate Mary's yes with a special feast day on March 25. We call this day the Feast of the Annunciation. **Annunciation** means "announcement." The Feast of the Annunciation helps us remember Gabriel's announcement to Mary.

We don't have to wait for a feast day to remember Mary's yes. We remember it every time we pray the Hail Mary. This prayer begins with the words Gabriel used to greet Mary.

PRAYER

With your classmates, pray the Hail Mary slowly. Think of what the words mean as you pray.

CHAPTER 5

The Father of Jesus

PRAYER

**Jesus, you tell us how to call God "Father."
Help us live as God's children.**

Richard's class had homework. The students had to write about special adults in their lives. This is what Richard wrote.

My Father
by Richard

My father is my best friend. He fixes things at home. He goes to work every day. He buys me things I need.

My father takes care of me. He keeps me safe. He shows me how to do things.

My father loves me, and I love him. I call him Daddy.

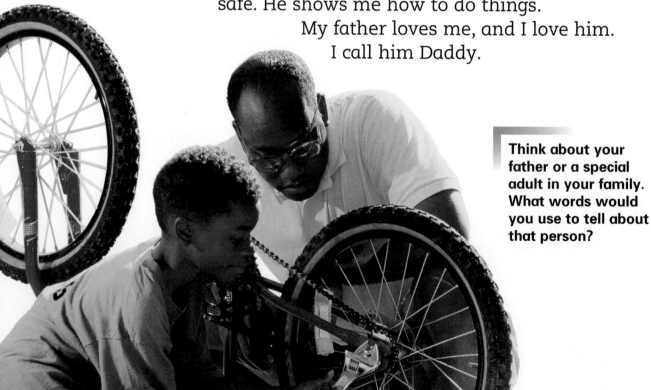

Think about your father or a special adult in your family. What words would you use to tell about that person?

A Good Relationship

Richard and his father are very special to each other. They love each other. They do things together. They have a good *relationship*.

Jesus had a good relationship with his Father, too. Jesus' Father is God.

All through his life, Jesus stayed close to his Father. He talked to God in prayer. Jesus chose to act in ways his Father would like. He did his Father's work in the world.

Jesus called God *Abba*. This is a word for a loving father. Today we might say "Daddy" or "Papa." He called God "my Father in heaven." **Heaven** is our word for life with God forever.

Jesus wants us to love his Father, too. Jesus used words and actions to show people that God is a loving parent. God cares for all people as his children.

Catholics Believe . . .

Jesus showed us that God is our Father.

Catechism, #240

ACTIVITY

Make a thank-you card for someone who loves and cares for you as God does.

Scripture Story
How to Pray

Our Moral Guide

Living as good followers of Jesus means trusting and obeying God. We do what God wants when we follow the commandments.

Catechism, #2072

How do we show that we trust and obey God?

One day Jesus told his followers how God wants us to live. "When you do good things, don't tell everyone," Jesus said. "Your Father in heaven will know what you have done. You don't need to show off!"

Jesus continued, "You don't have to pray in a loud voice, either. God, your Father, is not far away. God hears you even when you speak in your heart, without words.

"Your prayers don't have to go on and on. People who pray long, loud prayers are not always talking to God. Sometimes they are only talking to themselves or showing off for others.

**"This is how you should pray:
Our Father in heaven, help us honor your name. . . ."**

—based on Matthew 6:1–9

The Lord's Prayer

We still use the prayer that Jesus taught his followers. We call it the **Lord's Prayer**. Sometimes the prayer is known by its first two words, "Our Father." All followers of Jesus pray these words. We all call God "Father."

This chart shows what the words of the prayer mean.

The Lord's Prayer	Meaning
Our Father in heaven, hallowed be your name;	We praise God, our Father. We say God's name with love and respect.
your kingdom come;	We want everyone in the world to care for and love one another.
your will be done on earth as it is in heaven.	We will do what God wants, not what we want.
Give us this day our daily bread;	We ask God to give us what we need for now.
and forgive us our trespasses as we forgive those who trespass against us;	We ask God to be as forgiving of us as we are of others.
and lead us not into temptation, but deliver us from evil.	We ask God to protect us from harm and keep us from sin.
Amen.	May it be so!

RECALL

What name did Jesus use for his Father in heaven?
What prayer did Jesus teach us?

THINK AND SHARE

What is one way you can show that you are a child of God?

CONTINUE THE JOURNEY

List three words that you would use to tell someone about God. Choose one word from your list, and draw a picture for it.

God is

_____

_____

_____

WE LIVE OUR FAITH

 At Home   Share what is meant by "Give us this day our daily bread." Pray the Lord's Prayer with your family at mealtime.

In the Parish   Find out about ways that your parish community shows we are children of God. How does your parish show love for God and others?

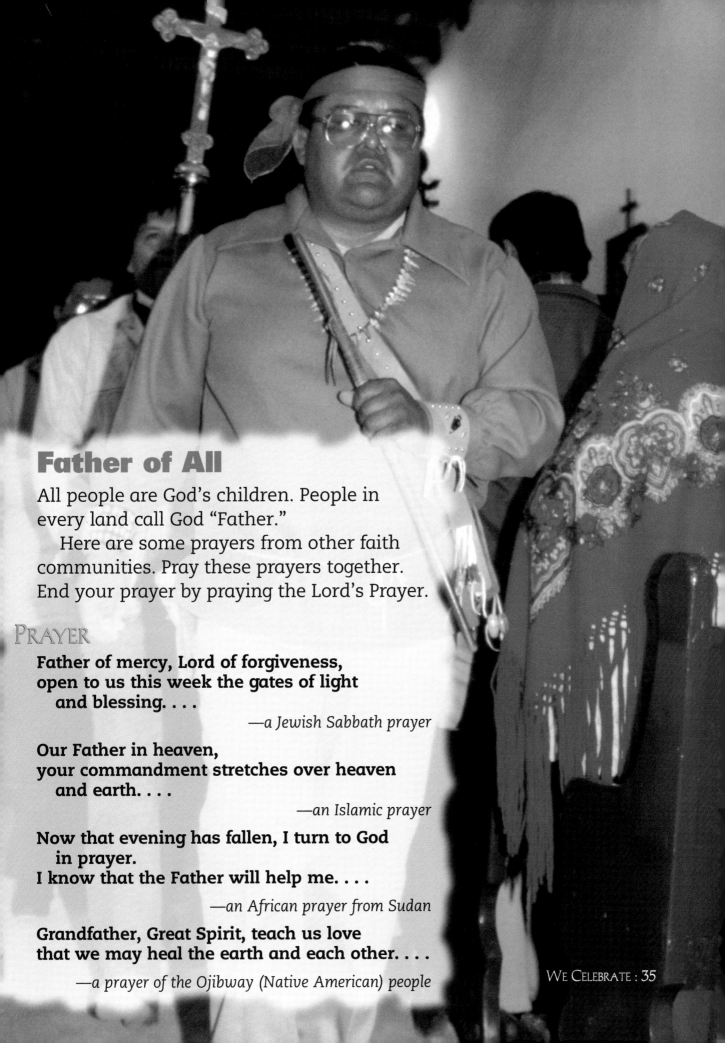

Father of All

All people are God's children. People in
every land call God "Father."

Here are some prayers from other faith
communities. Pray these prayers together.
End your prayer by praying the Lord's Prayer.

PRAYER

**Father of mercy, Lord of forgiveness,
open to us this week the gates of light
and blessing. . . .**

—a Jewish Sabbath prayer

**Our Father in heaven,
your commandment stretches over heaven
and earth. . . .**

—an Islamic prayer

**Now that evening has fallen, I turn to God
in prayer.
I know that the Father will help me. . . .**

—an African prayer from Sudan

**Grandfather, Great Spirit, teach us love
that we may heal the earth and each other. . . .**

—a prayer of the Ojibway (Native American) people

CHAPTER 6

God Gives Us Life

PRAYER

God, you have given us many signs of your love. We thank you for sharing your life.

A famous singer likes to talk about her childhood. "I spent every weekend with my grandmother. I called her *Abuela*. She picked me up on Friday night. My bag was packed and I was ready to go. I remember how she gave me a big hug. Even when I got older, that hug felt good.

"Abuela always had my favorite foods on hand. We played games together, and we ate lots of ice cream.

"My grandmother paid attention to me. She sat through my long stories. She listened to my problems. She gave me advice.

"When I got home, I sometimes found a note from Abuela in my bag. This was another sign of her love for me."

● **What are the signs of love in this story?**

ACTIVITY

Make up a story about the singer and her grandmother. What signs of love does the girl show her grandmother?

The Gift of Grace

There are many signs of God's love in our world. God gives us the gifts of creation. God gives us human life. God watches over us. But God gives us even more.

God gives us a wonderful gift. This gift is God's own life. God shares his life with us in the loving relationship called **grace**. God's own Son, Jesus, makes it possible for us to share in God's grace.

We celebrate our relationship with God in the **sacraments** of the Church. When we celebrate the sacraments, we remember Jesus. We grow in our love of God and others. Through the action of Jesus we receive God's gift of grace in the sacraments. The sacraments make God's life stronger in us and make us a better people.

The first sacrament we receive is **Baptism**. In Baptism we become members of the Church. The priest or *deacon* says, "I baptize you in the name of the Father, and of the Son, and of the Holy Spirit."

ACTIVITY

Draw a picture of your Baptism. Include the people who were there to welcome you into the Church.

Celebrating Grace

There are seven sacraments. Each one celebrates the gift of God's grace. Each one helps us grow in God's love.

This chart shows the seven sacraments.

The Sacraments

	Sacrament	What It Celebrates
Initiation	Baptism	We become members of the Church.
	Confirmation	The Holy Spirit strengthens us.
	Eucharist	We receive the Body and Blood of Jesus.
Healing	Reconciliation	We show that we are sorry for our sins. We receive God's forgiveness and the grace to do better.
	Anointing of the Sick	God's grace strengthens us in times of sickness, old age, and death.
Service	Matrimony	A man and a woman promise to love each other for life.
	Holy Orders	A man answers God's call to serve God and the Catholic community as a deacon, priest, or bishop.

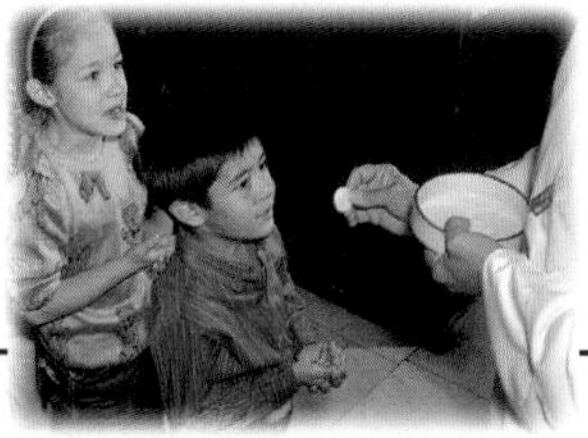

SCRIPTURE STORY

Paul's Message

When he was a young man, Paul did much to hurt the followers of Jesus. But one day God changed his life forever. Paul became a follower of Jesus. He was baptized.

Paul traveled around telling everyone about Jesus. Paul sent letters to the first Christians. He wrote about God's grace.

"God has been so kind to me!" Paul wrote. "God gave me the gift of grace. I have God's life in me, but it's not so I can show off. I am not an important person at all. But God chose me to tell everyone about Jesus. Because you follow Jesus, God's grace is given to you, too!"

—based on Ephesians 3:7–8

Our Moral Guide

The grace of the sacraments helps us follow the way of Jesus.

Catechism, #2003

What have you seen people doing to follow Jesus? What will you do to be a follower of Jesus?

The letters that Saint Paul wrote are sometimes called *epistles.* Some of them are collected in the Bible. We hear readings from these letters at Mass.

RECALL

What do we call the gift of loving relationship with God? How does the Church celebrate this relationship?

THINK AND SHARE

Think about the gift of grace. What can you do to thank God for this gift?

CONTINUE THE JOURNEY

Draw a picture of yourself being a sign of love to others.

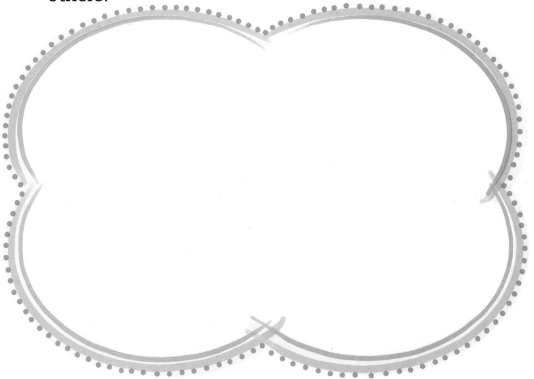

WE LIVE OUR FAITH

 At Home   Ask a family member or godparent to share memories of your Baptism.

In the Parish   Visit your parish church. Ask someone to explain the prayers, actions, and objects used in the Sacrament of Baptism.

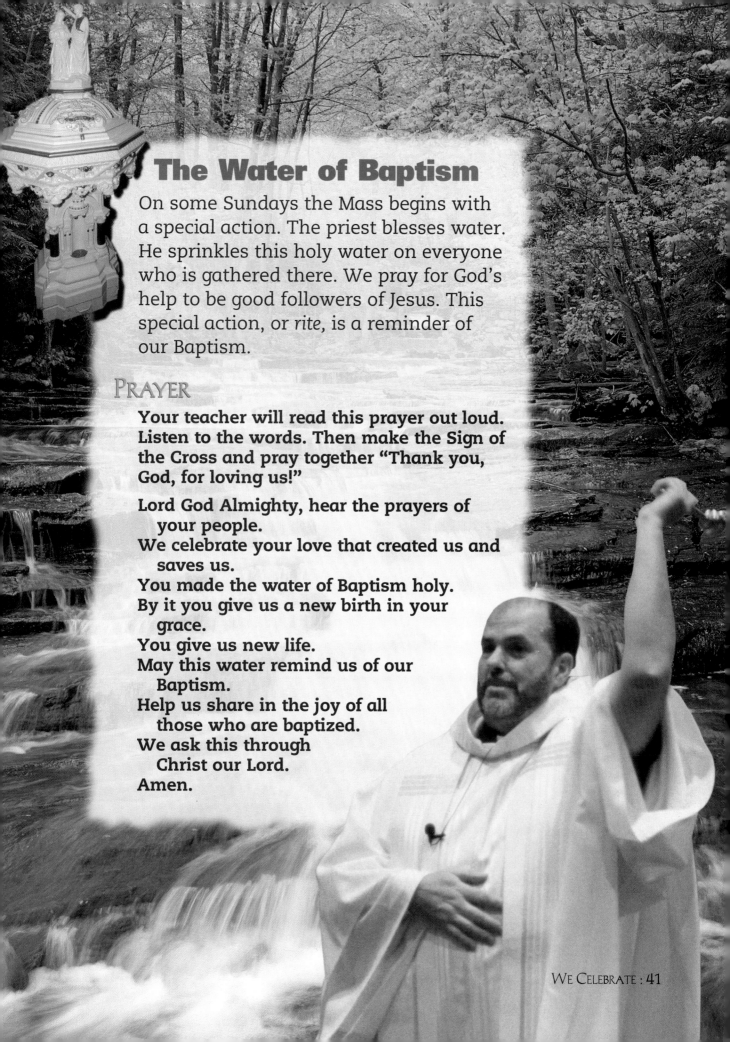

The Water of Baptism

On some Sundays the Mass begins with a special action. The priest blesses water. He sprinkles this holy water on everyone who is gathered there. We pray for God's help to be good followers of Jesus. This special action, or *rite*, is a reminder of our Baptism.

PRAYER

Your teacher will read this prayer out loud. Listen to the words. Then make the Sign of the Cross and pray together "Thank you, God, for loving us!"

Lord God Almighty, hear the prayers of
  your people.
We celebrate your love that created us and
  saves us.
You made the water of Baptism holy.
By it you give us a new birth in your
  grace.
You give us new life.
May this water remind us of our
  Baptism.
Help us share in the joy of all
  those who are baptized.
We ask this through
  Christ our Lord.
Amen.

CHAPTER 7

The Holy Spirit Is with Us

PRAYER

Holy Spirit, you bring us God's grace. Help us love the people who are with us.

ACTIVITY

Matt will miss Sam when he moves. Write a postcard from Sam to Matt. Have Sam tell Matt about his new home.

What if you had to move to another state? You might have to stay there for a long time. You would miss your friends, and they would miss you.

How would you keep in touch with your friends? Would you send them letters? Could you call them on the phone?

Jesus spent years with his friends. He taught them about God. He showed them how to love each other.

The time came for Jesus to return to his Father in heaven. But Jesus promised to be with his friends forever. How did Jesus stay in the lives of those who believed in him?

SCRIPTURE STORY
Jesus' Promise

Why did Jesus promise to ask his Father to send the Holy Spirit?

Jesus' friends were sad. He had returned to heaven to be with his Father. Jesus' friends felt lonely.

They gathered together. They shared a meal, and they told stories. They remembered the night before Jesus died.

"We were sad then, too," Peter said. "But do you remember what Jesus told us?"

John smiled. "Yes," he said. "Jesus told us we would never be alone. He promised to ask his Father to send us a Helper. That Helper is the **Holy Spirit**."

Soon Jesus' friends felt better. They remembered Jesus' promise. They waited together for the coming of the Holy Spirit to help them learn what was good and true. They knew the Holy Spirit would always be with them as a sign of Jesus' love.

—based on John 14:16–17

Scripture Signpost

"I will send you the Spirit who comes from the Father and shows what is true. The Spirit will help you and will tell you about me."

John 15:26

What kind of help do we need from the Holy Spirit?

Father, Son, and Holy Spirit

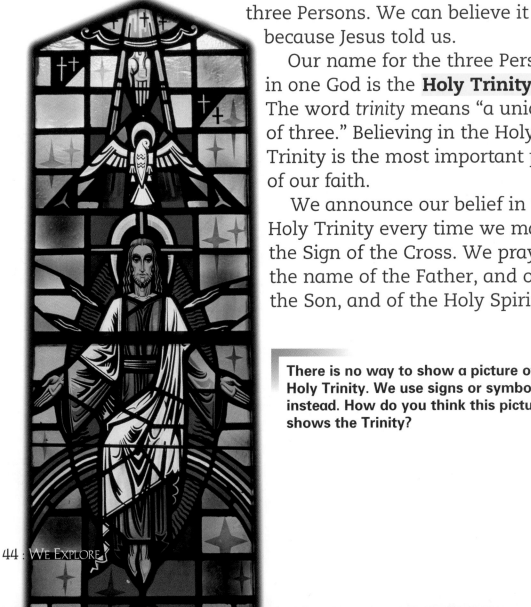

Catholics Believe . . .

that every part of our Christian life is connected to the Holy Trinity.

Catechism, #259

Jesus taught us something special about who God is. From Jesus we learn that God is our Father. We know that Jesus, the Son of the Father, is also God. And the Holy Spirit, sent from the Father and the Son, is also God.

But there are not three gods. There is only one God, who is Father, Son, and Holy Spirit. How can this be?

God is bigger than our words. We can't explain everything that we believe about God. But we can believe in one God who is three Persons. We can believe it because Jesus told us.

Our name for the three Persons in one God is the **Holy Trinity**. The word *trinity* means "a union of three." Believing in the Holy Trinity is the most important part of our faith.

We announce our belief in the Holy Trinity every time we make the Sign of the Cross. We pray "in the name of the Father, and of the Son, and of the Holy Spirit."

There is no way to show a picture of the Holy Trinity. We use signs or symbols instead. How do you think this picture shows the Trinity?

Asking for God's Help

One reason we pray is to ask for God's help. You can make up your own *petition,* or asking prayer.

Here are steps to follow:

- Begin by calling on God. You can say "God our Father," "Dear Jesus," or "Holy Spirit."

- Keep God's loving actions in your mind. You can say "God, you love us," "Jesus, you teach us," or "Holy Spirit, you help us."

- Ask God to help you with something you need. You might say "Help me be more patient."

- Add any other things you want to say to God. Use your own words.

- End your prayer. One way to end a prayer is to say "Through Jesus Christ, our Lord. Amen."

Where Will This Lead Me?

When you make up your own prayers, you can talk to God from your heart as a friend.

RECALL

Who is the Helper Jesus promised to send? Who is the Holy Trinity?

THINK AND SHARE

How can we show that the Holy Spirit is with us?

CONTINUE THE JOURNEY

Draw your own sign for the Holy Trinity.

WE LIVE OUR FAITH

At Home   Make up an asking prayer for something your family needs. Pray it with your family.

In the Parish   At Mass, listen for prayers and readings that talk about the Persons of the Trinity.

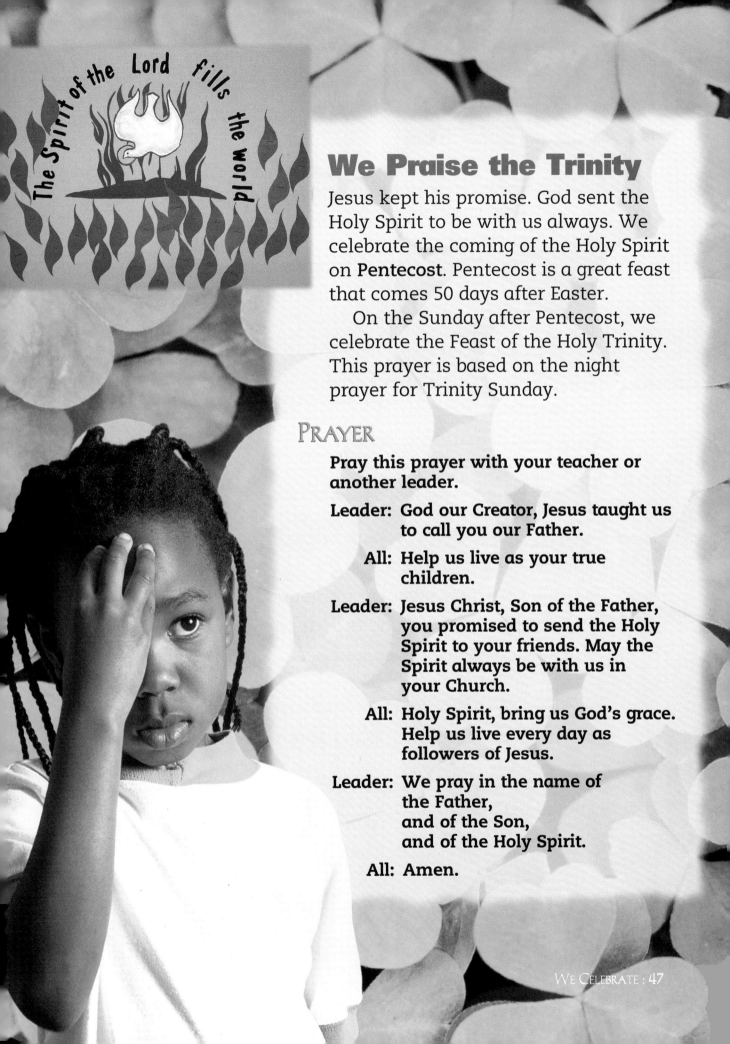

The Spirit of the Lord fills the world

We Praise the Trinity

Jesus kept his promise. God sent the Holy Spirit to be with us always. We celebrate the coming of the Holy Spirit on **Pentecost**. Pentecost is a great feast that comes 50 days after Easter.

On the Sunday after Pentecost, we celebrate the Feast of the Holy Trinity. This prayer is based on the night prayer for Trinity Sunday.

PRAYER

Pray this prayer with your teacher or another leader.

Leader: God our Creator, Jesus taught us to call you our Father.

All: Help us live as your true children.

Leader: Jesus Christ, Son of the Father, you promised to send the Holy Spirit to your friends. May the Spirit always be with us in your Church.

All: Holy Spirit, bring us God's grace. Help us live every day as followers of Jesus.

Leader: We pray in the name of the Father, and of the Son, and of the Holy Spirit.

All: Amen.

Review

Matching   Match the meanings in Column A with the correct terms in Column B.

Column A

_____ 1. The gift of God's own life in us.

_____ 2. The first sacrament we receive.

_____ 3. One God who is Father, Son, and Holy Spirit.

_____ 4. The name Jesus used for God, his Father.

_____ 5. The prayer Jesus taught us.

Column B

a. *Abba*

b. grace

c. Holy Trinity

d. the Lord's Prayer

e. Baptism

Which Is Correct?   Circle the correct term to complete each sentence.

1. There are (ten, seven) sacraments.

2. Jesus promised to send the (Father, Holy Spirit).

3. The Lord's Prayer is sometimes called the (Hail Mary, Our Father).

4. Through the sacraments, God gives us (grace, the Bible).

5. The Holy Spirit is our (King, Helper).

Share Your Faith   Someone asks you, "How should people pray?" What do you say?

Show How Far You've Come
Use the chart below to show what you have learned. For each chapter, write or draw one important thing you remember.

Jesus Teaches Us About God

Chapter 5 The Father of Jesus	Chapter 6 God Gives Us Life	Chapter 7 The Holy Spirit Is with Us

What Else Would You Like to Know?
List any questions you still have about the Father, Son, and Holy Spirit.

_____

_____

Continue the Journey
Choose one or more of the following activities to do on your own, with your class, or with your family.

- Look through your Faith Journal pages for Unit Two. Choose your favorite activity, and share it with a friend or family member.

- Make a poster or mural of the seven sacraments. Show signs of each sacrament or pictures of people celebrating each sacrament.

- Make a welcome card or plan a welcoming party for people in your parish who have recently been baptized.

Stars for God

PRAYER

**Saints of God, you are happy in heaven.
Help us follow your example and shine like
stars with God's love.**

Have you ever seen a champion gymnast? Have you ever watched a very good dancer?

Some people become really good at doing something. Some people become good musicians. Others become sports stars. Some people are very good teachers or writers or doctors. How do people become good at something?

Some people become really good at loving other people and God. We call these people **saints**. The word *saint* means "holy one." Saints live with God in heaven. In life they were ordinary people. But they became good at sharing God's love. They became stars for God.

ACTIVITY

Think of something you enjoy doing. Pretend you are the best in the world at doing it. Describe how you got to be a star.

We are all called to be saints.

Models to Follow

In some ways saints are like other kinds of stars. No one gets to be good at something without a lot of practice. Musicians and sports stars practice for many hours. Saints practice all through their lives.

Saints grow in **holiness**, or living as God wants us to live. Praying, learning about Jesus, celebrating the sacraments, and sharing with others are all ways to grow in holiness.

Many people want to be like famous sports stars or musicians. These stars can be good *role models*, or people to follow. As Christians we want to be like the saints. They are our role models.

But saints are different from other kinds of stars, too. Some stars are not good models. They may be good singers or players, but they do not always live good lives. Saints always show us how to live as God wants.

Sometimes other kinds of stars can be selfish. They think they are the best in the world and don't need anyone else. Saints know that no one can be a star alone. Really being the best in the world means being unselfish. It means sharing with others. It means loving God more than anything.

Catholics Believe . . .

that the saints are models who show us how to love God and others.

Catechism, #2030

RECALL

What does the word *saint* mean? What is holiness?

THINK AND SHARE

What are some ways we can practice becoming saints?

CONTINUE THE JOURNEY

For each letter in the word SAINTS, think of a term that describes saints. The letter *I* has been done for you.

S _____

A _____

I n heaven with God _____

N _____

T _____

S _____

WE LIVE OUR FAITH

At Home Tell a family member how saints are like other stars. Also explain how saints are different from other stars.

In the Parish Find out something about the saint your parish is named after. If your parish name is not a saint's name, find out about any saints whose pictures you find in your church.

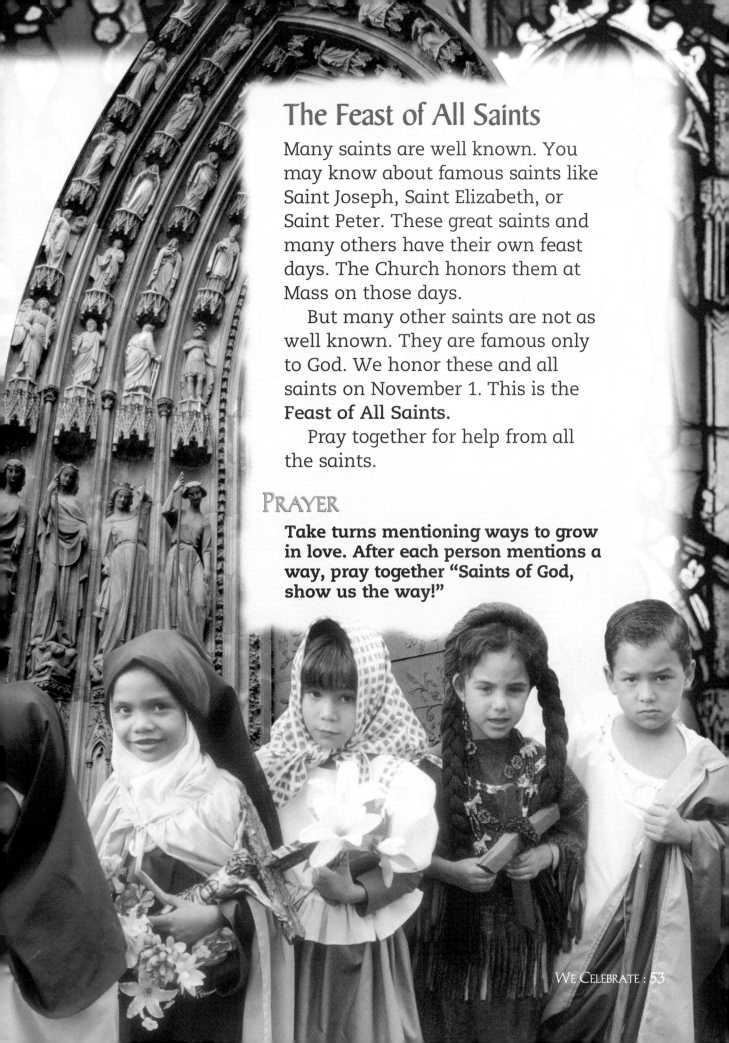

The Feast of All Saints

Many saints are well known. You may know about famous saints like Saint Joseph, Saint Elizabeth, or Saint Peter. These great saints and many others have their own feast days. The Church honors them at Mass on those days.

But many other saints are not as well known. They are famous only to God. We honor these and all saints on November 1. This is the **Feast of All Saints.**

Pray together for help from all the saints.

Prayer

Take turns mentioning ways to grow in love. After each person mentions a way, pray together "Saints of God, show us the way!"

CHAPTER 9

Jesus Shows Us How to Love

PRAYER

Jesus, help us follow you in all we do. Lead us to your heavenly Father.

Kim woke up excited. This was the day of the theme park trip.

Then Kim's mom came into the room. She looked worried.

"Honey, I'm sorry," Kim's mom said. "I have some bad news. Aunt Beverly was in an accident. She's going to be all right, but I have to go to the hospital to be with her. You can still go on the trip. Or you can come with me.

Kim thought for a minute. She didn't want to miss the trip. But her aunt was more important.

"I'll go with you," Kim said. "And I'll draw a get-well picture for Aunt Beverly."

- If you were Kim, what would you choose to do? Why?

Making a Choice

We can't always have our own way. We may have to give up something we want so others can have what they need.

Giving something up for a loving reason is called making a **sacrifice**. No one can force us to make a sacrifice. It is our choice.

SCRIPTURE STORY
Follow Me

It seemed like just another day of fishing for the two men. Simon and his brother Andrew spent the day in their boat. They threw the nets into the water. The sea was full of fish, and soon the nets were heavy.

Simon and Andrew sailed back to shore. There they saw a man watching them.

"That's Jesus," Andrew told his brother. "He goes around teaching people about God."

Just then Jesus called out to them. "Come with me! You are good at gathering lots of fish. But if you follow me, we will gather people instead."

Andrew and Simon looked at each other. They looked at Jesus and smiled. They left their fishnets and their boat and walked off down the beach with Jesus.

—based on Mark 1:16–18

Our Moral Guide

As followers of Jesus we are called to give up everything that keeps us from doing what God wants.

Catechism, #1723

What kinds of things do we have to give up when we choose to follow Jesus?

What did Simon and Andrew sacrifice in order to follow Jesus?

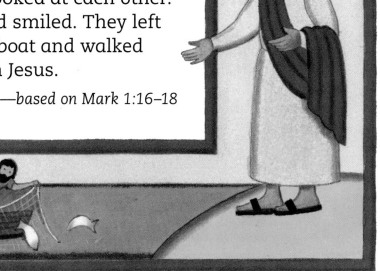

Following Jesus

Simon, whom Jesus called *Peter*, and his brother Andrew were the first people to follow Jesus. Many others joined them. They went with Jesus from town to town. They listened to Jesus' stories about God's love. They watched Jesus heal sick people and forgive sinners.

The men and women who chose to follow Jesus are called his **disciples**. The word *disciple* means "learner." The disciples did not just study what Jesus had to say. They tried to follow his example in every action. Like Jesus, the disciples told people about God's love. They reached out to people who were sick or sad. They made sacrifices to help others.

Jesus made the greatest sacrifice of all. He gave his life for us on the cross. He still calls people to follow him. Today we are Jesus' disciples.

Landmark The cross is a sign of Jesus' sacrifice. Wearing a cross is a way to tell the world "I am a follower of Jesus." We should back up this sign with our words and actions.

Making a Sacrifice

When we give up something we want so we can help someone else, we are living as Jesus lived. Making sacrifices is not easy. But practicing this kind of giving helps us grow in love.

Here are steps to follow when you are faced with a choice:

- Pay attention to the other person. Listen to what the person is saying. Find out what the person needs.

- Think about what Jesus would do.

- Think of something you can do for the person. Be sure it is something you are able to do. Think of yourself doing this with love.

- Understand what you will be giving up. Ask yourself, "Am I willing to make this sacrifice?"

- Ask the Holy Spirit for help.

- Decide what you will do, and do it.

Where Will This Lead Me?

Making loving sacrifices will help you see that other people's needs are important. This will make you less selfish. It will make you a better follower of Jesus.

RECALL

What does it mean to make a sacrifice? What do we call the followers of Jesus?

THINK AND SHARE

How can we show that we are Jesus' disciples?

CONTINUE THE JOURNEY

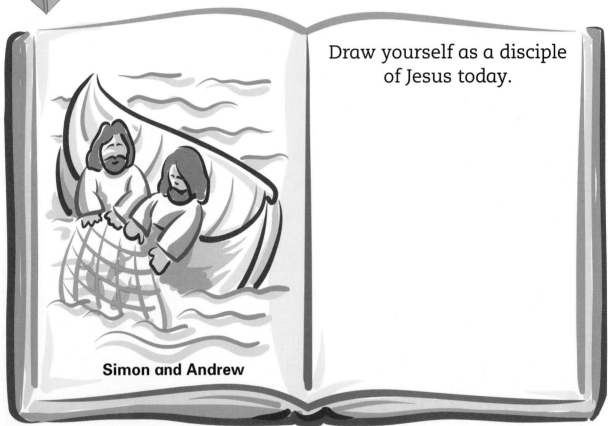

Simon and Andrew

Draw yourself as a disciple of Jesus today.

WE LIVE OUR FAITH

At Home Talk with family members about what it means to make a sacrifice. What sacrifices do family members make for one another?

In the Parish Ask three people in your parish community what it means to be a disciple. How do the people of your parish help others?

For Love of You

In the sacrifice of the Mass, Jesus *offers*, or gives, himself to the Father. We offer ourselves to God, too.

To show that we love God, we can pray a *morning offering*. This prayer says that we give every minute of every day to God. When we do this, we promise not to live just for ourselves. We try to do everything out of love, as Jesus did.

Pray this prayer together.

PRAYER

**Dear God, you have given us everything.
Now we give ourselves to you.
We offer you every thought,
every word, and every action of this day,
all for love of you.
Accept our sacrifice, we pray,
through Christ our Lord.
Amen.**

CHAPTER 10

Jesus Feeds Us

PRAYER

**Jesus, you give us everything we need to live.
Thank you for being the bread of life for us.**

What's your favorite food? How often do you eat this food? Why is it your favorite?

You may like some foods better than others. But you know we need all kinds of food to live. Food gives energy to our bodies and helps us grow.

Parents feed their children. People offer food when friends visit. Sharing food is part of many good times in our lives.

Our bodies aren't the only parts of us that need to be fed. Food can feed our hearts, too. Sharing food is a sign of love and care.

ACTIVITY

Make up a story about what these children are celebrating. What are some other times when we celebrate by sharing a meal?

Jewish families still celebrate the Sabbath meal each week, as Jesus' family did.

Jesus Shared Meals

Jesus knew how important food was to people. He fed hungry people. He shared meals with his friends. The Gospels contain many examples of how Jesus used mealtimes to teach people about God's love.

Meals were holy times for Jesus. He celebrated the Jewish **Sabbath**, the weekly time of prayer. The Sabbath began with an evening meal. As a young boy Jesus watched his mother light the Sabbath lamps. He heard his foster father bless the Sabbath bread and wine. And every year Jesus and his family celebrated the feast of *Passover* with a special meal.

When Jesus grew up, he shared these holy meals with his friends. Jesus knew that whenever people share meals and love, God is there with them.

Catholics Believe . . .

that Jesus fed hungry people as a sign of God's saving love.

Catechism, #549

I Am the Bread of Life

Scripture Signpost

The people said, "Lord, give us this bread and don't ever stop!"

John 6:34

We were very hungry. We had been listening to Jesus all day. His words about God's love were wonderful. But it was getting late. Our stomachs were rumbling.

The nearest town was more than an hour away. Some people had food, but there wasn't nearly enough to go around. There were hundreds and hundreds of people!

Jesus saw the problem. He told his friends to buy some food from the people who had it and share it with everyone.

"We only have a few coins!" Jesus' friends said. "We can't feed all these people!"

Jesus called to a young boy who was selling food. The boy had only five loaves of bread and two dried fish. But he gladly gave them to Jesus.

Jesus blessed the bread and fish. Then he gave the food to his friends. They started breaking it into pieces and passing it to the crowd.

Something wonderful happened. The bread and fish never ran out! We all had enough to eat. And there were twelve baskets of leftovers! It was a **miracle**, a powerful sign of God's love.

"This is like what happened years ago!" someone called out. "Our people were lost in the desert. They were hungry. They prayed, and God sent them **manna**, food from heaven."

Jesus spoke in a loud voice. "Yes," he said. "Our people ate manna in the desert. But it did not last forever. Today real bread from heaven has come. I am the Bread of Life that comes from God. Whoever eats this bread will never be hungry again. This bread brings life that lasts forever."

Jesus' words were difficult. But we tried to understand what he meant. With Jesus our hearts are filled with God's love.

—based on John 6:1–40

Saints Walk with Us

Saint Elizabeth of Hungary
Feast Day: November 17

Elizabeth was rich. She always shared her family's food with hungry people.

Saint Elizabeth is usually shown carrying bread and roses. Like Jesus, she shared food as a sign of God's love.

ACTIVITY

Make a reminder of Jesus' words. Draw a picture of a loaf of bread. On it, write *I am the Bread of Life.*

RECALL

What is a miracle? Who called himself "the Bread of Life"?

THINK AND SHARE

Why do we say that mealtimes are holy times?

CONTINUE THE JOURNEY

Draw yourself sharing a meal with Jesus.

WE LIVE OUR FAITH

 At Home Make decorated place mats for a family meal. Lead your family in a prayer of blessing or thanks for the food you have.

In the Parish Look for ways your parish community shares food. How can you join in?

Meal Prayers

Jesus always blessed food before sharing it. He gave thanks to God, his Father, for every meal.

Followers of Jesus also bless food and thank God. Pray these meal prayers together before and after a meal or snack.

PRAYER

Blessing Before Meals

**Bless us, O Lord, and these your gifts
which we are about to receive
from your goodness.
Through Christ our Lord.
Amen.**

Thanksgiving After Meals

**We give you thanks for all your gifts,
almighty God,
living and reigning now
and for ever.
Amen.**

CHAPTER 11

Jesus Forgives Us

PRAYER

Jesus, you forgive our sins. Thank you for your great love for us.

"I'm sorry, Daddy," Steven said softly. "What I did was wrong."

Steven looked into his father's eyes. He saw his father's gentle smile. "All right, Son," Steven's father said. "Now go to your sister. Tell her you're sorry."

Steven felt bad about stealing his sister's birthday money. He went to find her.

"I'm sorry, Emily," Steven said. "I won't ever do that again. I'll pay you back from my allowance. And I'll do your chores for a week."

Emily was still upset. But she knew Steven meant what he said. "Okay, Steven," Emily said. "I forgive you."

What did Steven do wrong? How will he make up for it?

ACTIVITY

Think about a time when someone forgave you. Write that person a thank-you note.

Forgiveness

We know what it feels like to do something wrong. When we hurt others, we hurt ourselves, too. When we have done something wrong, we feel cut off. We want to return to a loving relationship.

Steven was sorry, and his father knew it. When his father forgave him, Steven felt loved. Then Steven asked Emily to forgive him, too. He promised to do better. He told Emily he would try to make up for what he had done.

We all do wrong things. We want to be forgiven. We want to start over. Jesus tells us that God, our loving Father, will always forgive us. God wants us to show that we are sorry for hurting others. God wants us to make up for what we have done.

God is full of **mercy**, or loving kindness. We can choose to ask for forgiveness. It's up to us. God's mercy and forgiveness are always there for us.

Catholics Believe . . .

that God is merciful and forgiving.

Catechism, #270

Signs of Mercy

Jesus did many things to show God's mercy. He healed people who were sick. He helped people whose minds were troubled. He forgave people for their sins.

Everywhere he went, Jesus called people to return to God's love. Jesus told special teaching stories, called **parables**. Many parables were stories about God's mercy and forgiveness. Here is one of those stories.

SCRIPTURE STORY

The Forgiving Father

Once a father had two sons. The younger son did not want to stay at home. "Give me my half of your money," the son said.

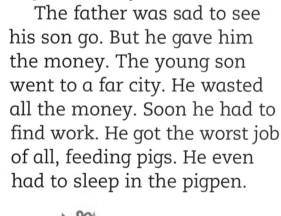

The father was sad to see his son go. But he gave him the money. The young son went to a far city. He wasted all the money. Soon he had to find work. He got the worst job of all, feeding pigs. He even had to sleep in the pigpen.

ACTIVITY

As a class, make up your own parable about God's mercy.

The son thought about how good his life had been at home. He felt sad. "I'll go home," the son thought. "I'll beg my father to give me a job as his servant."

Scripture Signpost

"The Father is a merciful God, who always gives us comfort."
2 Corinthians 1:3

How does God show us mercy?

The son started out for home. While he was still far off, the son saw his father running toward him. It was as if his father had been waiting for him all along. The son said, "I have sinned, Father. I'm not good enough to be your son."

The father hugged his son. He led him home and dressed him in fine clothes. He threw a big party.

The older brother was puzzled. "Why are we having a party?" he asked. "I stayed with you. He hurt you. But he gets the party!"

The father hugged his older son. "I love you," he said. "You are special to me. But it's as if your brother had died, and he has come back to life. He found his way home. So we celebrate."

Both brothers learned what a loving father they had.

—*based on Luke 15:11–32*

- **What do you think people learned about God when Jesus told this story?**

RECALL

What is mercy? What do we call the special teaching stories Jesus told?

THINK AND SHARE

Why do we feel sad when we do something wrong?

CONTINUE THE JOURNEY

Think of a time when you did something wrong. Write a short prayer. In your own words, ask for God's forgiveness.

_____

_____

_____

_____

_____

_____

_____

_____

WE LIVE OUR FAITH

At Home Practice mercy in your family. Forgive family members who ask your forgiveness.

In the Parish Join in the *penitential rite* at the beginning of the Mass, when we remember God's mercy.

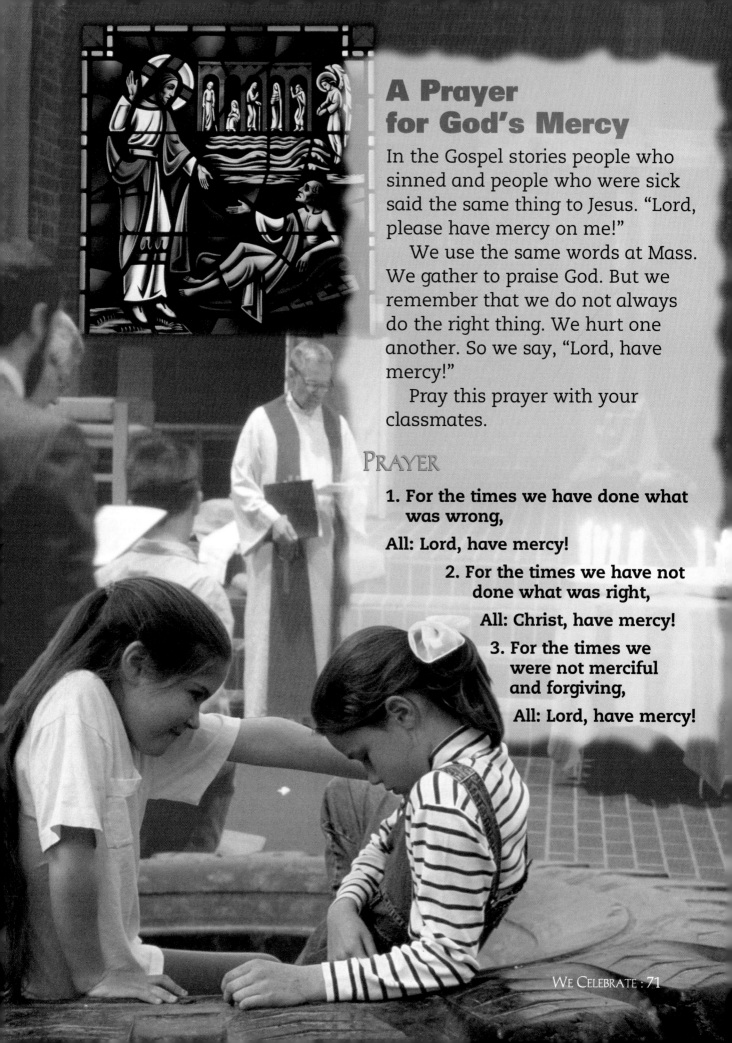

A Prayer for God's Mercy

In the Gospel stories people who sinned and people who were sick said the same thing to Jesus. "Lord, please have mercy on me!"

We use the same words at Mass. We gather to praise God. But we remember that we do not always do the right thing. We hurt one another. So we say, "Lord, have mercy!"

Pray this prayer with your classmates.

Prayer

1. For the times we have done what was wrong,

All: Lord, have mercy!

2. For the times we have not done what was right,

All: Christ, have mercy!

3. For the times we were not merciful and forgiving,

All: Lord, have mercy!

Review

Fill in the Blanks Choose the correct term from the word bank to complete each sentence.

1. Giving up something to help others is called making

   a _____.

2. The followers of Jesus are called _____.

3. A _____ is a powerful sign of God's love.

4. Jesus taught people about God's loving kindness,

   or _____.

5. Jesus used special teaching stories called

   _____.

Word Bank

disciples   mercy   miracle   parables   sacrifice

Who Am I? Match each description in Column A with the correct person in Column B.

Column A

_____ 1. I fed many people with only five loaves of bread.

_____ 2. Jesus called me Peter.

_____ 3. I shared my family's riches with people who were poor.

_____ 4. My brother Simon and I left our fishnets to follow Jesus.

_____ 5. I forgave my son when he returned.

Column B

a. Simon

b. the forgiving father

c. Andrew

d. Jesus

e. Saint Elizabeth of Hungary

Share Your Faith Tell the parable of the forgiving father in your own words.

Show How Far You've Come
Use the chart below to show what you have learned. For each chapter, write or draw one important thing you remember.

Jesus Shares Himself with Us

Chapter 9 Jesus Shows Us How to Love	Chapter 10 Jesus Feeds Us	Chapter 11 Jesus Forgives Us

What Else Would You Like to Know?
List any questions you still have about what Jesus taught us.

_____

_____

_____

Continue the Journey
Choose one or more of the following activities to do on your own, with your class, or with your family.

- Look through your Faith Journal pages for Unit Three. Choose your favorite activity, and share it with a friend or family member.
- Read or listen to a book that tells one of Jesus' parables. Then tell the story to someone else in your own words. Tell what you think the story means.
- Plan a special meal for your family, your friends, or your religion class. Make up a blessing prayer for your meal.

Come, Lord Jesus!

PRAYER

**Come, Lord Jesus! Come into our lives.
Come into our homes. Come into our hearts.**

People do many things to get ready for Christmas. Families get together to prepare for the holiday.

Our Church family prepares for Christmas, too. This time of preparing is called **Advent**. The word *Advent* means "coming." During Advent we get ready to celebrate the coming of Jesus.

The Season of Advent lasts for four weeks before Christmas. Our Church family prepares by sharing special readings, prayers, and customs. We remember that Jesus was born in Bethlehem. We are glad that Jesus is with us now in the Eucharist. And we look forward to the end of time, when Jesus will come again.

What are some things your family does to prepare for Christmas?

Prepare the Way

Getting ready for Christmas is not only preparing presents. We need to prepare our hearts, too. We need to get ready for the coming of Jesus.

Long ago God chose prophets to call people back to him. A **prophet** is someone who brings God's message to people. The prophets said, "Prepare the way of the Lord! Make a straight path where there used to be a crooked road. Then everyone will see God's power." The prophets meant that people should straighten out their lives.

SCRIPTURE STORY

John's Message

Jesus' cousin John was a prophet. John lived in the desert. He ate only a little food. He wore clothing made from animal skin. John trusted God to take care of him. When John came out of the desert, he announced that a Savior was coming. People asked John how they should prepare for the Savior's coming. John told them:

> "Turn back to God and be baptized! Then your sins will be forgiven. If you have two coats, give one to someone who doesn't have any. If you have food, share it with someone else."
> —based on Luke 3:3–11

Jesus' cousin is known as *Saint John the Baptist*. John was called the *baptist* because he baptized people. John baptized Jesus in the Jordan River.

RECALL

What is Advent? Who was the prophet who baptized people and told them how to prepare for the Savior?

THINK AND SHARE

How can we do what John told people to do?

CONTINUE THE JOURNEY

Draw something you can do to prepare for the coming of Jesus.

WE LIVE OUR FAITH

 At Home   With your family, plan things you can do to prepare your hearts for Christmas. Do one thing each week of Advent.

In the Parish   Listen carefully to the Advent readings at Mass. Listen for the story about John the Baptist.

A Sign of Promise

Our Catholic family has many Advent customs. An *Advent calendar* is one way to count off the days until Christmas. Each day of the calendar has a door to open. Behind each door is a picture or a prayer.

Lighting the candles of the *Advent wreath* is another custom. We light one more candle each week during Advent. The green branches of the wreath remind us that God gives us life. The candles remind us that Jesus is the Light of the World, who lights up our hearts.

Pray the Advent wreath blessing together.

Prayer

Lord God,
   let your blessing come upon us
as we light the candles
   of this wreath.
May the wreath and its
   light
be a sign of Christ's promise
   to bring us salvation.
May he come quickly and not
   delay.
We ask this through Christ
   our Lord.
Amen.

CHAPTER 13

The Church Is a Community

PRAYER

Jesus, we believe in you. We want to follow you. Help us be a loving community.

Jennifer walked up the steps of her new school. She held her mom's hand. She felt nervous because she didn't know anyone.

Jennifer and her mom saw a large banner above the door. It read "Saint Michael's School—A Community of Love and Learning."

"What's a community, Mom?" asked Jennifer.

"A **community** is a group of people, Jennifer. These people share something in common. The children and teachers in your new school are a community. They come together to learn new things."

As she walked into her new school, Jennifer began to feel better.

The people in a community have something in common. What do the members of your class have in common? How is your class a community?

Followers of Jesus

The **Church** is also a community. The Church is made up of people who believe that Jesus is the Son of God. We follow the way of Jesus in what we say and do.

Most people in the Catholic Church belong to a **parish**. A parish is a community of love and worship. The people of the parish believe in Jesus. We care for each other. We worship God together at Mass.

Catholic schools and parish schools of religion are communities within a parish. They are communities where people learn together, worship together, and care for each other.

Catholics Believe . . .

that the Church is a community of people gathered by God to follow Jesus.

Catechism, #752

People gather together for Mass at their parish church. What is the name of your parish? How is it a community?

The First Christians

ACTIVITY

Act out an example of how Christians today care for one another.

It was a special day for the followers of Jesus. They had told the story of Jesus to the people of Jerusalem. About three thousand people asked to be baptized. The people wanted to be a part of the Christian community.

The first Christians were like family to each other. They often met together and shared everything they had. They sold their belongings and gave the money to whoever needed it. They shared their food happily and willingly. Day after day they met in the Temple. A *temple* is a building where people **worship**, or pray to God together as a community. The first Christians prayed in the Temple and celebrated the Eucharist in their homes.

—*based on Acts 2:41–47*

• **What did the first Christians do as a community that showed they were followers of Jesus?**

Church Leaders

God calls certain people to be *leaders* of our Church. A leader is someone who helps and guides other people. Working with other people, leaders *respond* to the needs of people in the community.

God calls many people to serve as parish leaders. These leaders help and guide others in many different ways. Someone hears God's call to lead the preschool program. Another person answers God's call to help feed those in need. Someone else answers the call to be the principal of a Catholic school or the director of religious education.

One person God calls is the **pastor**. The word *pastor* really means "shepherd." The pastor is a priest who leads and cares for the parish as a shepherd cares for a flock of sheep.

Saints Walk with Us
Saint John Vianney
Feast Day: August 4

Saint John Vianney was the pastor of a small country parish in France. He gave good advice to everyone.

Saint John Vianney is the patron saint of parish priests.

Who is the pastor of your parish? How does he serve the members of your parish?

RECALL

What is a community? What do we call the community where we celebrate Mass?

THINK AND SHARE

What can second graders do to help the parish community?

CONTINUE THE JOURNEY

In the picture of the parish church, write the names of people who lead and serve your parish community.

WE LIVE OUR FAITH

At Home Tell your family what you know about the first Christians. Then follow the first Christians' example by sharing what you have with other family members.

In the Parish With a family member, look through a copy of your parish bulletin. Find out how your parish community serves the needs of people in your area.

Prayer of Support

God calls people to serve the Church as leaders. We support our leaders by praying for them.

Pray this prayer together. Fill in the names of the Church leaders you know.

PRAYER

O God, you call men and women
   to serve as leaders in the Church.
Hear our prayers for (*Name*), our
   pastor, and (*Name*), our teacher.
May they always look to Jesus as the
   example of a good leader.
May the Holy Spirit guide them
   as they serve our community.
   Amen.

CHAPTER 14

Doing the Work of Jesus

PRAYER

Jesus, help us follow you. Help us share your love with others.

What if your favorite basketball player asked you to join the team? What if the best children's book author chose you to draw the pictures for a new book?

When you *admire* someone, you want to do what he or she does. You want to be a good follower.

The Church is made up of people who love and follow Jesus. As members of the Church community, we show our love by continuing the work of Jesus.

Look at the pictures. Think about what Jesus did when he was on earth. Then tell how the people in the pictures are doing the work of Jesus.

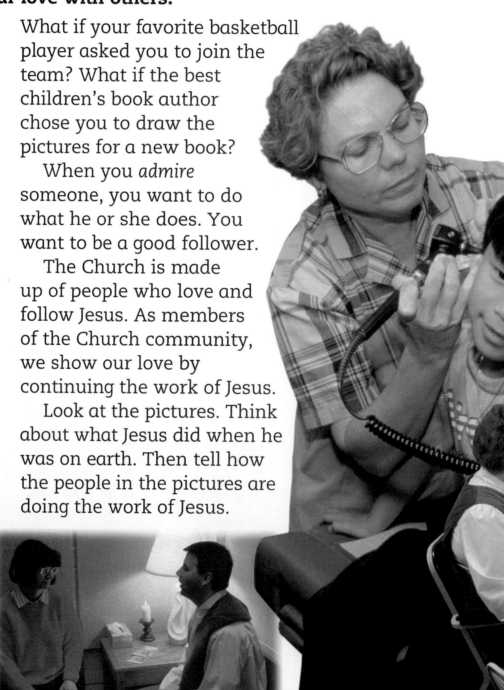

Landmark The good news of Jesus was first brought to the Americas by missionaries from Spain and France. This picture shows the oldest Catholic parish church in the United States. The parish was begun by Spanish missionaries more than 450 years ago in St. Augustine, Florida.

We Are Sent

Jesus helped people in need. He forgave people's sins. He showed people the way to God.

The Church continues the work of Jesus. This is the mission of the Church. The word **mission** means "the work we are sent to do." Jesus sends each of us, just as he sent his first followers, to do his work. We all take part in the mission of the Church.

Sometimes we do Jesus' work right where we are. Sometimes the followers of Jesus are sent to other countries to carry out their mission. People who bring the good news of Jesus to far lands are called **missionaries**.

Catholics Believe . . . all members of the Church share in its mission to spread God's kingdom.

Catechism, #863

Scripture Signpost

"The good news is spreading all over the world with great success."

Colossians 1:6

How have you told someone about Jesus lately?

Everyone Is Called

God calls all people to life and happiness with him. The Church spreads this good news. All the members of the Church are called to do Jesus' work in their everyday lives. All have different gifts. Each one has a special way to serve. Some members are involved in **ministry**, or service, in the Church.

Some men are called to the Sacrament of Holy Orders. They do the work of Jesus as bishops, priests, and deacons. They are called *ordained* ministers. Bishops lead a group of parishes. A priest leads a parish in worship and service. A **deacon** works with the priest in meeting the needs of the parish.

Most men and women serve the Church as *lay people.* Lay ministers read the Scriptures and lead the singing at Mass. They teach religion classes and prepare people for the sacraments. They visit the sick and comfort the lonely.

Some people serve God by getting married and raising children. They love each other and teach their children to love. They have celebrated the Sacrament of Matrimony. Others serve God as single people. Some single Catholics serve as *religious sisters and brothers.*

ACTIVITY

Make a list of ways families can do the work of Jesus.

We are all called to help in the Church's mission. Remember that you are not too young to do God's work. Here are some ways you can help.

Doing Our Part

Where Help Is Needed	What We Can Do
At home	• Tell a younger brother or sister about Jesus. • Pray with family members. • Forgive and ask forgiveness of others. • Respect and obey parents and others who care for us.
In school	• Treat others as Jesus would treat them. • Help others get along peacefully. • Learn about the world God made and the people who are our brothers and sisters.
In the parish	• Participate at Mass. • Get to know our parish ministers. Support their work. • Share time, talent, and money. • Learn about, and pray for, missionaries from our area.

RECALL

What is the mission of the Church? What does the word *ministry* mean?

THINK AND SHARE

Why do you think the Church needs all its members to do Jesus' work?

CONTINUE THE JOURNEY

Draw one way the Church carries out Jesus' work today.

WE LIVE OUR FAITH

 At Home From the chart on page 87, choose one of the ways to serve at home. Practice it this week.

In the Parish Find out some things lay people do in the parish to continue the work of Jesus. Make and send cards thanking people for their service.

Pray for Others

At Mass we pray for the needs of people around the world. We pray for our parish and our community. These prayers are called the *general intercessions*.

Take turns praying these intercessions. After each one, pray together "Lord, help us do your work."

PRAYER

Let us pray to God, who cares for all.
   Lord, help us do your work.
Bless the people of the Church. . . .
Guide the rulers of nations. . . .
Support all families. . . .
Protect the unborn. . . .
Be a helper to the poor. . . .
Give health to the sick. . . .
Protect the elderly. . . .
Forgive sinners. . . .
Protect and bless all ministers
   and missionaries. . . .
Show us how to share love and
   bring good news. . . .

CHAPTER 15

The Church Remembers Jesus

PRAYER

Jesus, you saved us through your sacrifice on the cross. We thank you and praise you forever.

Ronald looked at the picture in the album. "Great-Grandpa, who's this?" he asked. Ronald's great-grandfather smiled. "That's me when I was a soldier. It was many years ago in Europe."

A sad look came across Great-Grandpa's face. He continued, "That was a painful time. Many young soldiers died. They sacrificed their lives."

Great-Grandpa quickly pointed to another picture. He said, "Here's one from a happier time. It shows me marching in the Memorial Day parade. We march every year to honor those who gave up their lives."

Ronald felt proud of his great-grandfather.

On Memorial Day we remember soldiers who died. *Memorial* **means "remembering." What other holidays help us remember people who make sacrifices for us?**

Why did Jesus offer his life for us on the cross?

Remembering Jesus' Sacrifice

Like Ronald, we also feel proud. We feel proud of Jesus because he sacrificed his life to set us free from sin.

Start

At Mass we gather as a community to remember Jesus' sacrifice on the cross. We think about all he did to save us. The Mass is our memorial of Jesus' love. We remember how Jesus gathered with his friends for the Last Supper. In the holy bread and wine, he shares his Body and Blood.

Jesus offered his life for us on the cross. At every Mass we join in his sacrifice.

The Mass is our celebration of the Sacrament of the **Eucharist**. The word *Eucharist* means "thanksgiving." When we celebrate the Mass, we thank God the Father for sending his Son to save us. We thank Jesus for his sacrifice. We thank the Holy Spirit for being with us always.

Catholics Believe . . .

that the Eucharist is a memorial of Jesus' sacrifice.

Catechism, #1366

The Worshiping Community

The Church is a worshiping community. It continues to offer Jesus' sacrifice in the Eucharist. When we come together for Mass, we are doing what the Church is meant to do.

The words and actions of the Mass are very important. They bring us closer to God and to one another.

At Mass we gather with other followers of Jesus. We sing and pray together. We listen to readings from the Bible. We offer gifts of bread and wine. We remember and give thanks. We receive Jesus in Holy Communion.

The priest stands in the place of Jesus at Mass. He offers our sacrifice of love and thanks to God. The deacon and other ministers help lead us in worship. But all of us celebrate the Eucharist together. Every person shares in Jesus' holy meal.

Our Moral Guide

The Eucharist brings all members of the Church together. It helps us grow in love.

Catechism, #1394, 1396

How can we show that we are *united* in the Eucharist?

ACTIVITY

Draw something you remember about the Mass. If you need help remembering the parts of the Mass, look at the outline on page 180.

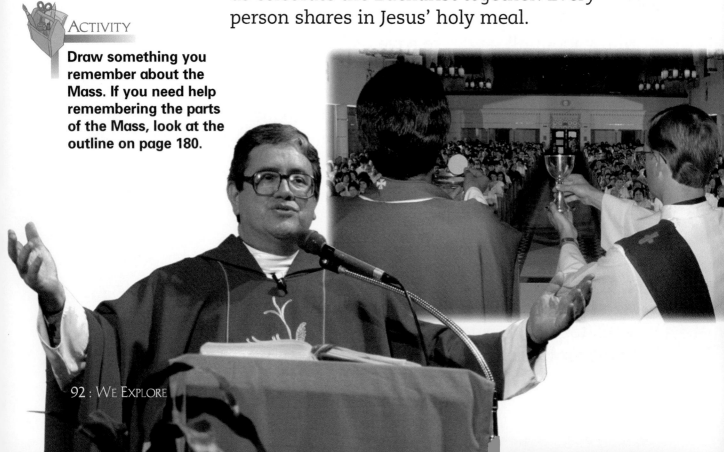

Taking Part in the Mass

When we take part in the Mass, we thank God for Jesus' loving sacrifice.

Here are some ways to join in the celebration:

- Get to know the parts of the Mass.

- Greet other members of the community.

- Show respect in the way you stand, sit, kneel, and bow.

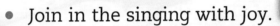

- Join in the singing with joy.

- Learn the prayers and responses. Think about the words when you pray aloud.

- Listen carefully to the Scripture readings and the *homily*.

- Follow the actions of the priest, deacon, and other ministers.

- Receive Holy Communion when you are able.

- Pray a silent prayer of thanks to God in your own words.

Where Will This Lead Me?

Learning how to take part in the Mass will help you join more fully in the Church's celebration of the Eucharist.

RECALL

How does the Church remember Jesus' sacrifice?
What does the word *Eucharist* mean?

THINK AND SHARE

Why is it important to know what is happening
at Mass?

CONTINUE THE JOURNEY

Write your own prayer thanking Jesus for
his sacrifice.

Eucharist   Thanksgiving

WE LIVE OUR FAITH

At Home Let your actions show that
you are thankful for Jesus' sacrifice. Make a
sacrifice to show family members that you
love them. Make up after any quarrels.

In the Parish Practice the steps for
taking part in the Mass.

We Remember

The central prayer of the Mass is called the *Eucharistic Prayer*. During this prayer we remember Jesus' sacrifice. The priest says, "Let us proclaim the mystery of faith." We answer with a short prayer called the *memorial acclamation*.

Pray each of these memorial acclamations aloud with your classmates. When you say the words, thank God in your heart for the gift of Jesus.

PRAYER

A. Christ has died,
   Christ is risen,
   Christ will come again.

B. Dying you destroyed our death,
   rising you restored our life.
   Lord Jesus, come in glory.

C. When we eat this bread and
      drink this cup,
   we proclaim your death,
      Lord Jesus,
   until you come in glory.

D. Lord, by your cross and
      resurrection
   you have set us free.
   You are the Savior of the world.

Review

Matching
Match the descriptions in Column A with the correct terms in Column B.

Column A

_____ 1. The sacrament that celebrates Jesus' sacrifice.

_____ 2. Someone who brings the good news of Jesus to another country.

_____ 3. A word that means "service."

_____ 4. The meal at which Jesus blessed bread and wine.

_____ 5. The priest who leads and cares for a parish.

Column B

a. Last Supper

b. ministry

c. missionary

d. Eucharist

e. pastor

Which Is Correct?
Circle the correct term to complete each sentence.

1. We gather to remember Jesus' sacrifice at (Mass, Memorial Day).

2. God calls some people to (lay, ordained) ministry as bishops, priests, and deacons.

3. Most people in the Catholic Church belong to a (missionary, parish).

4. The Church is a (community, club).

5. The Church's (pastor, mission) is to continue Jesus' work.

Share Your Faith
Someone asks you to explain how the Church is a community. What do you say?

Show How Far You've Come

Use the chart below to show what you have learned. For each chapter, write or draw one important thing you remember.

Jesus Lives in the Church

Chapter 13 The Church Is a Community	Chapter 14 Doing the Work of Jesus	Chapter 15 The Church Remembers Jesus

What Else Would You Like to Know?

List any questions you still have about the Church as a community that follows Jesus.

_____

_____

_____

Continue the Journey

Choose one or more of the following activities to do. You can do these on your own, with your class, or with your family.

- Look through your Faith Journal pages for Unit Four. Choose your favorite activity, and share it with a friend or family member.

- Make a booklet with prayers and responses used at Mass. Use your booklet to help you take part in the Mass more fully.

- Make a poster that shows how your parish community continues the work of Jesus.

Jesus Is Born

PRAYER

**Jesus, we remember your birth in Bethlehem.
We praise God for your coming!**

What do you like about birthdays? What things do you like to do on your birthday?

On Christmas Day we celebrate the birth of Jesus. We celebrate God's becoming human in Jesus. Christmas is also called the Feast of the **Nativity**. The word *nativity* means "birth."

We recall that Jesus was born in a stable in Bethlehem. We remember the love of Mary and Joseph. We joyfully celebrate the coming of the Son of God.

Christmas is a special time. It is a time for love and prayer.

 ACTIVITY

**Plan a celebration in honor of Jesus' birth.
What would you do to make the celebration a happy event?**

Peace on Earth

On the night when Jesus was born, some shepherds were guarding their sheep on a hillside.

An angel came to the shepherds with good news. At first they were frightened. But the angel said, "Don't be afraid. A Savior has been born tonight. You will find him in Bethlehem, in a stable."

Suddenly the whole night sky seemed full of angels. "Glory to God in the highest!" the angels sang. "And peace on earth to everyone who pleases God."

The shepherds got up right away. They all went to Bethlehem. The shepherds found Baby Jesus with Mary and Joseph. They praised God.

—based on Luke 2:8–20

Catholics Believe . . .

that Jesus, the Son of God, was born in a simple stable. We celebrate his birth on Christmas Day.

Catechism, #525

● **What gift did God give all people? Why do you think we give gifts at Christmas to people we love?**

ACTIVITY

Pretend you were with the shepherds on the first Christmas. In your own words, tell what happened.

RECALL

What do we celebrate on the Feast of the Nativity? Where was Jesus born?

THINK AND SHARE

What can we do to celebrate Christmas as the birth of Jesus?

CONTINUE THE JOURNEY

Draw a gift you would give Jesus in honor of his birth.

WE LIVE OUR FAITH

 At Home This Christmas, give family members the gift of your loving actions.

In the Parish Join with your parish community at Mass to celebrate the Feast of the Nativity on Christmas Eve or Christmas Day.

Peace on Earth

Peace is another gift we receive at Christmas. **Peace** is the quiet, happy feeling we have when we are safe and loved.

We can share the gift of peace at Christmas and every day. When we help others feel peaceful, we are saying thank you to God for this gift.

With your classmates, pray this Christmas prayer. Then sing a Christmas carol about the gift of peace, such as "Silent Night."

PRAYER

Lord Jesus,
in the peace of the Christmas Season,
   our hearts are happy.
With animals and angels,
   with shepherds and stars,
   with Mary and Joseph we sing
    God's praise.
Through your birth
   may all people find peace.

CHAPTER 17

Jesus Invites Us to Love

PRAYER

Jesus, you loved God the Father. You loved all people. Help us follow your example of love.

Dear Beth,

Hi! I really miss you! How is your new school? Do you have any new friends? I am fine. Do you remember Anna? Well, we are really good friends now. Can you believe it?

It happened after my dad had a talk with me. He wanted to know why Anna and I weren't friends anymore. I told him how Anna told my brother I rode his bike. That made me mad! I decided never to talk to Anna again.

But my dad said that wasn't the right thing to do. He said that I should treat Anna the way I would want her to treat me. I think my dad's right. Wish you were here.

Write soon!

Love,

Rebecca

ACTIVITY

Think of a time when you did not treat someone else the way you would want to be treated. Then draw a picture showing how you could have acted differently.

When Rebecca's dad told her to treat Anna as she would like Anna to treat her, he was talking about the *Golden Rule*. The Golden Rule says to treat others just as you want to be treated.

Jesus taught the Golden Rule. He said that following this rule helps us show our love for other people.

Catholics Believe . . .

that Jesus calls us to live by the Golden Rule.

Catechism, #1970

We Live by Laws

Laws, or rules, help people live together in peace. They help people be fair and kind. What are some of the laws in your community?

Jesus knew of God's love for him. In response to that love, he followed God's laws. He obeyed the **Ten Commandments**. *Commandment* is another word for law. The Ten Commandments tell us to put God first, respect life, respect parents, be truthful, and treat others fairly. The commandments help people show their love for God and for one another by doing the right thing.

What laws are these people following? Why do you think laws are important?

The Great Commandment

Saints Walk with Us

Saint Maximilian Kolbe
Feast Day: August 14

Maximilian was a priest who loved God very much. During a terrible war he was put in prison. He gave up his life to save another prisoner.

This is a painting of Saint Maximilian. He died in Poland in 1941.

Jesus taught people that God loved them. Whenever people asked Jesus what God wanted them to do, he had one answer. "Love God more than everything else," Jesus said. "And love others as you love yourself."

We call this teaching of Jesus the **Great Commandment**. It combines all the other commandments into one.

Jesus also gave us a list of ways to be truly happy and loving. We call these ways the **Beatitudes**. The word *beatitude* means "blessing." The Beatitudes say:

Depend on God.

Show mercy.

Make peace.

Do what is right,
    even if it is hard.

Jesus told us to love everyone, not just those who love us. He told us to ask forgiveness when we hurt someone.

The kind of love Jesus wants us to show is not just a feeling. It is a way of living. Our love for God and others needs to be put into action every day.

SCRIPTURE STORY
Love One Another

A follower of Jesus named John wrote a letter to a group of early Christians. John wanted to remind them of Jesus' teachings.

Our Moral Guide

We should love God above all things and love others as we love ourselves.

Catechism, #2055

What does it mean to love others as we love ourselves?

"My dear friends," John wrote, "I am not writing to give you a new commandment. You already know what Jesus wants us to do. From the very beginning we were told to love one another.

"Children, our love for each other has to be shown by how we live. It's not enough just to talk about it.

"We must love each other. Love comes from God. No one has ever seen God. But if we love each other, God lives in us. That's who God is— nothing but love.

"If we say we love God, but we don't love each other, we're lying. The commandment God has given us is not hard to follow. Love God and love each other!"

—*based on the First Letter of John*

How are these children showing love?

RECALL

What is a commandment? What is the Great Commandment?

THINK AND SHARE

Why is it important to show love in our actions?

CONTINUE THE JOURNEY

Write or draw one thing you will do this week to show that you follow both parts of the Great Commandment.

Love God

Love Others

WE LIVE OUR FAITH

 At Home Have a family meeting to make a list of family rules. Hang the list where everyone can see it.

In the Parish Find out how your parish shows love for people in need. Do what you can to help.

Praising God's Law

God loves us very much. We want to show love for God in return. God gives us the Ten Commandments and other laws to help us show our love.

Pray this prayer of thanks for God's law.

PRAYER

Our LORD, you bless everyone
    who lives right and obeys your law.
You bless all those who follow your
    commands from deep in their
    hearts.
You have ordered us always to obey
    your teachings.
We don't ever want to stray from
    your laws.
We will do right and praise you
    by learning to respect your perfect
    laws.
Show us your love and save us, LORD,
    as you have promised.

—based on Psalm 119:1–7, 41

CHAPTER 18

We Make Choices

PRAYER

Dear God, you gave us free will. Help us choose what is right.

Robert carried the shopping basket into the checkout line. His mother began to place the groceries on the counter.

It was then that Robert noticed the $20 bill on the floor. "Someone must have dropped it here," he thought.

Robert's mother continued to empty the basket. The cashier was busy checking the grocery items. Robert bent down and picked up the money.

- If you were Robert, what would you do next?

ACTIVITY

Pretend you are Robert's friend. Tell him what you think he should do.

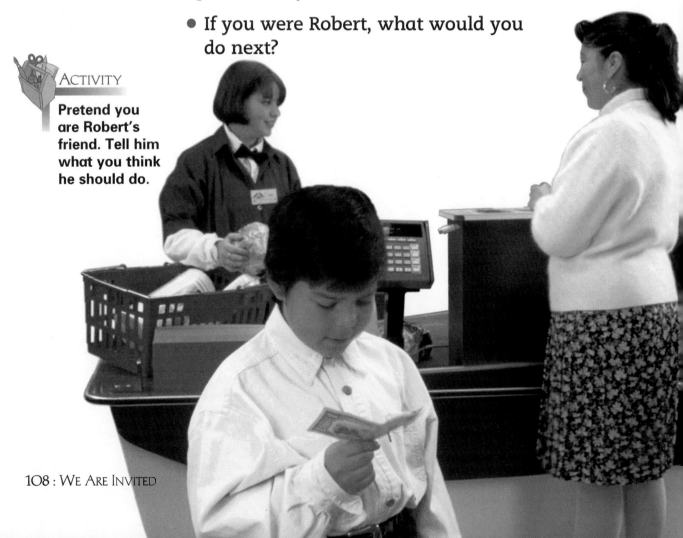

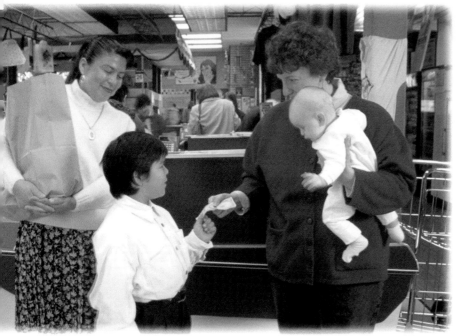

ACTIVITY

Make up a different ending to the story. What if Robert had decided to keep the money? What might have happened to the mother and her child?

Choosing What Is Right

Every day we make choices. What are some choices you make during the day?

Some choices are simple, like what to eat for lunch. Other choices are between what is right and what is wrong. These more serious choices are called **moral** choices. We know something is right when it follows God's law. We know something is wrong when it goes against our love of God and others.

God gives us the freedom to make moral choices. If we choose what is right, we act in a *responsible* way. We grow closer to God. We grow closer to others in the community.

Robert had a moral choice to make. Should he keep the $20 even though it did not belong to him? Robert decided that it was not right to put the money in his pocket. He started to give the $20 bill to the cashier.

Just then a young mother returned with her baby. She had dropped the money. When she saw the money, she smiled. The mother thanked Robert for being so honest.

Catholics Believe . . .

that we can choose between right and wrong. Choosing what is right brings us closer to God. Choosing what is wrong leads us to sin.

Catechism, #1732

Choosing What Is Wrong

Our Moral Guide

In order for sin to be mortal, three things must happen. The choice must be seriously wrong. You must know that it is seriously wrong. And you must freely choose it anyway.

Catechism, #1857

What actions do you think are seriously wrong?

We sin when we choose to say no to God's love and God's law. We sin when we choose to do what we know is wrong.

Some wrong choices are not sins. They are mistakes. We don't mean to hurt someone or to break God's law. We cannot sin by accident. It is only when we know something is wrong and we freely choose it anyway that we sin.

Some sins are very serious. When we freely choose to turn away from God's love completely, our choice is called **mortal** sin. The word *mortal* means "deadly." Mortal sin cuts us off from God's own life.

Most sins are **venial**. Venial sins are less serious than mortal sins. They come from bad habits or from laziness. They come from not paying attention to God's loving call. Venial sin does not cut us off completely from God's friendship and grace.

When we are sorry for sin, we can always ask for God's forgiveness. God's love for us never ends.

What choice did this child make? Tell whether you think this choice is a sin. Explain your answer.

Making Good Choices

God calls us to make good choices. God gives us the gift of **conscience**, which is the ability to tell the difference between right and wrong.

Here are some steps to follow as you make moral choices:

- Think about your choice before you act.

- Ask yourself, "What is the right thing to do?"

- Think about the results of your choice. Who will be helped? Who will be hurt?

- Ask yourself how Jesus would choose.

  - Compare your choice with the Great Commandment. Does your choice show real love for God, self, and others? Or does it show only selfishness?

  - Does your choice help you follow the Ten Commandments and the Beatitudes? Or does it break these laws?

  - If possible, talk about your choice with a family member or teacher. Get good advice about what the Church teaches.

- Ask the Holy Spirit for help in choosing what is right.

Where Will This Lead Me?

Learning to make good moral choices now will help you all through your life. It will help you grow in love for God and others.

RECALL

What is a moral choice? What gift from God helps us choose between right and wrong?

THINK AND SHARE

Explain the difference between mortal sin and venial sin.

CONTINUE THE JOURNEY

Trace the paths that lead to *Love*.

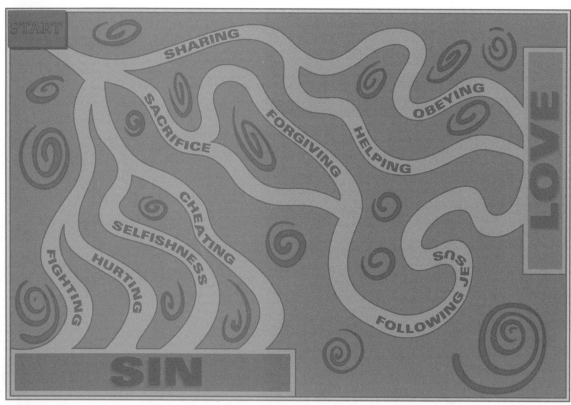

WE LIVE OUR FAITH

 At Home Talk with family members about how to make good moral choices.

In the Parish Join in the penitential rite at Mass. These prayers ask God to forgive our sins and help us choose what is right.

Spirit of God, Lead Us!

We pray to God for help in making good moral choices. We follow the example of Jesus. We ask the Holy Spirit to lead us.

Pray together for God's help.

PRAYER

God our Father,
you sent Jesus to be the friend of children.
He came to show us
    how we can love you, Father,
    by loving one another.
He came to take away sin,
    which keeps us from being friends,
    and hate, which makes us all unhappy.
He promised to send the Holy Spirit,
    to be with us always
    so that we can live as your children.
God the Father, Son, and Holy Spirit, be with us
    always and help us choose what is right!

—based on Eucharistic Prayer 2 for Masses with Children

CHAPTER 19

We Celebrate Forgiveness

PRAYER

Jesus, as the Son of God, you forgave sinners. We thank you for your love and forgiveness.

Think about a time when you asked someone to forgive you.

What wrong did you do? How did you feel about doing wrong?

Why did you ask for the person's forgiveness? How did you know you were forgiven? How did you feel after being forgiven?

Only God can forgive sins. God calls us to ask forgiveness. We ask God and the community for this forgiveness in the Sacrament of Reconciliation.

ACTIVITY

Make up a story about the girl on the left. Be sure forgiveness is part of your story.

The first step in asking God's forgiveness is contrition. **Contrition** is the sorrow we feel when we know we have done wrong. Contrition makes us want to heal our friendship with God. It makes us want to do better in the future.

SCRIPTURE STORY

The Woman Who Was Sorry

One day Jesus was having dinner at the home of a man named Simon. A woman came into the room where they were eating. Everyone knew that this woman was a sinner.

The woman was full of contrition. She was crying so hard she couldn't even speak. She went right to Jesus and sat on the floor by his feet. The woman washed the dust from Jesus' feet with her tears. She carefully dried his feet with her long hair. She put sweet-smelling oil on his feet, the way a servant would treat a king.

Simon and his friends were surprised. Didn't Jesus know what a sinner this woman was?

Jesus knew the woman was very sorry for her sins. Her actions showed this. Jesus said to the woman, "Your sins are forgiven. Because of your faith, you are now saved. May God give you peace!"

—*based on Luke 7:36–39, 48–50*

The Sacrament of Reconciliation

Catholics Believe . . .

that the Sacrament of Reconciliation celebrates our return to relationship with God and the community.

Catechism, #1468–1469

The Church celebrates God's forgiveness in the Sacrament of Reconciliation. The word *reconciliation* means "coming back into relationship."

In the Sacrament of Reconciliation, we *confess*, or tell, our sins to the priest. The priest acts in the place of Jesus. The priest may never tell anyone our sins. By confessing we admit that we have done wrong.

The priest may give us some advice about making better choices. Then he gives us a penance to do. **Penance** is a way of making up for the wrong we have done.

The priest says the words of absolution. **Absolution** means "washing away." When the priest absolves us, our sins are forgiven, and we make a new start.

If we have committed mortal sin, we must receive the Sacrament of Reconciliation before we can receive Communion again. We are not required to confess venial sins, but it is a good habit to get into.

The *Rite,* or ceremony, of Reconciliation can be celebrated in different ways. We can receive the Sacrament of Reconciliation individually or as part of a parish celebration.

Examining Your Conscience

To prepare for the Sacrament of Reconciliation, examine your conscience. Reflect on your thoughts, words, and actions. Remember Jesus' teachings about loving God and loving other people. See if your actions match the example Jesus gave us.

Ask yourself these questions:

- How have I done what God asks of me?

- When have I hurt a friend or family member?

- When have I failed to help someone in need?

- How am I working to be a better person?

- How am I trying to change bad habits?

You may want to talk with the priest about some of these questions when you confess your sins. Ask the Holy Spirit to help you celebrate the Sacrament of Reconciliation faithfully.

Where Will This Lead Me?

Examining your conscience will help you prepare for the Sacrament of Reconciliation. It will also help you learn to make better choices.

RECALL

What do we call the sorrow we feel when we have done wrong? What is penance?

THINK AND SHARE

Why do we need to receive the Sacrament of Reconciliation when we have committed mortal sin?

CONTINUE THE JOURNEY

Draw a picture of yourself receiving the Sacrament of Reconciliation.

WE LIVE OUR FAITH

At Home   Get in the habit of examining your conscience at the end of each day. As part of your night prayer, ask God to forgive any venial sins. Ask the Holy Spirit to help you improve.

In the Parish   Look at the steps in the Sacrament of Reconciliation on page 181. On a small card, list the steps in the sacrament. Add notes to remind you about what you are to do. Take the card with you when you receive the Sacrament of Reconciliation.

Prayer of Contrition

In the Sacrament of Reconciliation, we pray a prayer of contrition. We tell God and the community that we are sorry for having sinned. We promise to do better.

In a communal celebration of Reconciliation, we pray a litany of contrition together. Take turns reading the petitions of this prayer. After each petition, pray together "But you love us and come to us."

PRAYER

God our Father,
sometimes we have not behaved as
   your children should.
But you love us and come to us.

We have given trouble to our
   parents and teachers. . . .
We have quarrelled and called each
   other names. . . .
We have been lazy at home and
   in school, and have not been
   helpful to our families. . . .
We have thought too much of
   ourselves and have told lies. . . .
We have not done good to others
   when we had the chance. . . .

—*from the Rite of Penance*

Review

Fill in the Blanks
Choose the correct term from the word bank to complete each sentence.

1. Another word for law or rule is _____.

2. Something we do to make up for the wrong we have done is a _____.

3. The _____ teaches us to treat others as we would want them to treat us.

4. We celebrate God's forgiveness in the _____ of Reconciliation.

5. Serious sins are called _____ sins.

Word Bank
commandment   Golden Rule

mortal   penance   Sacrament

Which Is Correct?
Circle the correct term to complete each sentence.

1. Sorrow for our sins is called (contrition, confession).

2. Less serious sins that hurt our relationship with God and others are called (mortal, venial).

3. Jesus' teachings about blessings are called the (Ten Commandments, Beatitudes).

4. The gift of God that helps us know the difference between right and wrong is called (conscience, penance).

5. In the Sacrament of Reconciliation, the priest acts in the place of (our parents, Jesus).

Share Your Faith
Someone feels sorry about his or her actions. What can you tell this person about God's forgiveness?

Show How Far You've Come

Use the chart below to show what you have learned. For each chapter, write or draw one important thing you remember.

The Sacrament of Reconciliation

Chapter 17 Jesus Invites Us to Love	Chapter 18 We Make Choices	Chapter 19 We Celebrate Forgiveness

What Else Would You Like to Know?

List any questions you have about God's forgiveness and the Sacrament of Reconciliation.

_____

_____

Continue the Journey

Choose one or more of the following activities to do. You can do these on your own, with your class, or with your family.

- Look through your Faith Journal pages for Unit Five. Choose your favorite activity, and share it with a friend or family member.

- Look up the Ten Commandments on page 178. Make a book or poster showing ways to follow the commandments.

- Make up your own prayer of contrition. Tell how sorry you are for wrongs you have done.

A Time of Sacrifice

PRAYER

Jesus, you sacrificed your life for us. Help us learn to sacrifice during Lent. Be with us.

Look at the pictures. What is happening?

The Church celebrates a special season called **Lent**. Lent is the 40 days before Easter. This is a time of prayer, sacrifice, and works of **charity**, or loving care for others.

During Lent we remember Jesus and how he suffered and died for us. In return we make sacrifices for Jesus. We look forward to Easter, when we celebrate Jesus' resurrection.

Ash Wednesday is the beginning of Lent. We are marked with ashes in the sign of a cross. The ashes are a sign of sorrow for sin.

Lenten Signs

We receive ashes on Ash Wednesday. The ashes say we want to be better followers of Jesus. The person giving out the ashes makes a cross on each person's forehead. The giving of ashes is a sacramental.

During the Season of Lent, we celebrate with many customs. *Customs* are special ways of doing things.

We eat special foods during Lent. Long ago people did not eat butter or other fats during Lent. They made bread from flour, water, and salt. In Germany bakers formed the bread into long ropes. They twisted the ropes of dough to look like people praying with folded arms. That's where pretzels come from!

Hot cross buns are another Lenten food. Since Lent comes in the spring, people make sweet cakes with spring fruits and nuts. They mark the cakes with crosses to remind them of Jesus.

Catholics Believe . . .

that during Lent we remember the life and suffering of Jesus.

Catechism, #1163

Do you know any other Lenten customs?

RECALL

What do we call the Church season that comes before Easter? On what day do we receive ashes?

THINK AND SHARE

Why is it good to make sacrifices during Lent?

CONTINUE THE JOURNEY

What are some things that you might sacrifice during Lent? Draw a picture of one of these things.

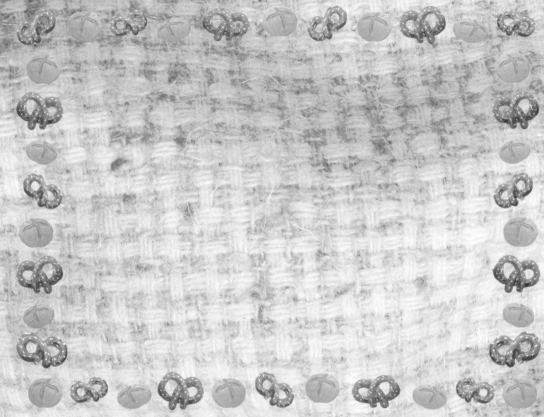

WE LIVE OUR FAITH

At Home Celebrate Lent by making or buying pretzels and hot cross buns as part of your family food.

In the Parish Look for signs that your parish community is celebrating the Season of Lent. Take part in your parish's celebration of Ash Wednesday.

We Sacrifice for Jesus!

During Lent we make sacrifices as we remember the sacrifices Jesus made for us. Choose one special thing you will give up or do during Lent. What you choose should show your love for God and others.

If you wish, share your sacrifice with the class. Dip your hand in holy water, and make the Sign of the Cross.

After the sharing, pray the prayer together.

PRAYER

O God, accept our sacrifices. By our words and actions during Lent, we want to draw closer to you. Amen.

CHAPTER 21

The Church Welcomes Us

PRAYER

Dear God, at Baptism you welcome us to a life of grace. We thank you for your love.

Pam walked into her new classroom. Everyone turned and stared. She didn't know anyone at all. "Where will I sit?" she thought, as her heart began to beat faster.

Just then, Mr. James, her new teacher, came to the rescue. "Welcome to your new class, Pam!" he said. "We're so happy you're here with us."

As Pam walked to her desk, she glanced at the faces of her classmates. Much to her surprise, some were smiling. One girl even waved as if to say "Hi!"

On her desk was a name card that said "Pam." There was also a small poster on which all the children had written their names. It read, "Welcome to our class!" Pam began to feel at home.

ACTIVITY

Pretend you are one of Pam's classmates. Make a list of the things you could do to make Pam feel welcome in her new school.

Which Sacraments of Initiation have you celebrated? Which Sacraments of Initiation will you celebrate in the future?

The Sacraments of Welcome

Pam was welcomed and accepted as a new member of her class. The teacher and the children made Pam feel like a part of their community.

The Church also welcomes people as new members. We celebrate this through the sacraments of welcome, which are Baptism, Confirmation, and the Eucharist. We call these the **Sacraments of Initiation**. *Initiation* means "beginning."

The Sacraments of Initiation help us grow in grace, God's life in us. Through Baptism we are welcomed into the Church community. In Confirmation the Holy Spirit strengthens us as followers of Jesus. When we celebrate the Eucharist, we thank God for sending Jesus.

The Sacraments of Initiation give us full membership in the Church. People who have not yet received these sacraments are called **catechumens**, or "learners." They are growing in knowledge of their faith.

Catholics Believe . . .

that the three Sacraments of Initiation are the basis of Christian life.

Catechism, #1212

Our Moral Guide

God calls on all Catholics to help young children grow in their faith.

Catechism, #1255

How do members of the Christian community help you learn about your Catholic faith?

Members of All Ages

Ordinarily, Catholics are baptized as infants. They celebrate First Eucharist at around the age of seven. And they may celebrate Confirmation some years later. Sometimes infants are baptized, confirmed, and receive Eucharist. Some children and most adults who become members of the Church celebrate the Sacraments of Initiation all at once.

When an infant is baptized, the child's parents promise to help their child grow in faith. Older children and adults make those promises for themselves. But no matter how old the person being baptized is, he or she does not stand alone. Besides the parents, infants and children have **godparents** to help them learn and live their faith. Older children and adults also have **sponsors** to carry out the same responsibility. People being confirmed have sponsors, too.

Godparents and sponsors stand for the whole Church community. Every member of the Church has the responsibility to help new members grow in faith and grace.

ACTIVITY

Imagine you could be a baby's godparent. Write or draw one thing you would like to tell the baby about Jesus.

Water and Spirit

We use natural things to celebrate every sacrament. The chart below shows the visible things used in Baptism. One very important baptismal sign can't be seen, but it can be heard. This sign is words. The words of Baptism must be said as the water is poured. Together the words and the water are the signs of the sacrament.

The priest or deacon says, "I baptize you in the name of the Father, and of the Son, and of the Holy Spirit."

The Sights of Baptism

Water is a sign of new life. It is a sign of washing and refreshment. In Baptism the priest or deacon pours water on the person's head. Sometimes the person is placed in the water.

The priest or deacon *anoints*, or rubs oils on, the person's head. Through anointing, the child shares in the life of Christ, the Anointed One. The Holy Spirit protects and strengthens the person.

White clothing is a sign of new life. A person being baptized wears white clothing or puts on a white cloth to show that he or she has begun a new life of grace.

A lighted candle is a sign of Christ, the Light of the World. The person is given a lighted candle as a sign that he or she shares the light of faith.

RECALL

What are the three Sacraments of Initiation? What are the signs of Baptism?

THINK AND SHARE

What do you think makes someone a good godparent or sponsor?

CONTINUE THE JOURNEY

Complete your own baptismal certificate. Decide what you will do as a Catholic Christian. Write in the spaces provided.

Baptismal Certificate

_____   _____
Name   Parish

"I promise to be a Catholic Christian by

_____

_____."

_____   _____
Date   Signature

WE LIVE OUR FAITH

 At Home   If possible, find out about each of your godparents. Ask each person why being a godparent is important.

In the Parish   Find out the names of people who are preparing to celebrate the Sacraments of Initiation in your parish. Pray for them.

We Promise, Lord!

Your parents and godparents may have made your baptismal promises, or **vows**, for you. But you can renew these promises yourself. The whole Church community renews baptismal promises every Easter.

Renew your promises as a class. Then, in your own words, thank God for the life of grace we share as members of the Church.

Prayer

Leader: Do you say no to sin?

All: We do!

Leader: Do you promise to turn away from what is wrong?

All: We do!

Leader: Do you promise to choose what is good?

All: We do!

Leader: Do you believe in God: Father, Son, and Holy Spirit?

All: We do!

CHAPTER 22

Jesus Is with Us

PRAYER

Jesus, we love you. We want to be with you always. Show us how to be close to you and to one another!

The morning went quickly for Pam in her new class. Soon it was lunchtime. The class started to form a line. Suddenly Pam heard Maria ask, "Want to eat lunch together?" "Sure," Pam answered with a smile.

Lunch with Maria was really fun. Some of the other children from the class sat with them. They told stories and laughed a lot.

When people share a meal together, something special can happen. They draw closer to each other. Often it is a time of celebration.

ACTIVITY

Make up a story about what these people are doing. What are they celebrating? What are they remembering?

We Share the Holy Meal

Jesus and his friends shared many meals. Later, when Jesus returned to his Father, he was still with his friends in their holy meal. Jesus is with us, too. He comes to us in a special way when we share the holy meal of the Eucharist.

SCRIPTURE STORY

The Last Supper

On the night before he died, Jesus shared a very special meal with his friends. He blessed and shared bread and wine.

"This bread is my Body," Jesus told them. "This wine is my Blood. Whenever you bless and share this meal, I will be there with you."

—based on 1 Corinthians 11:23–26

At Mass the priest does as Jesus did. He **consecrates**, or makes holy, the bread and wine. Then he shares it. And Jesus is with us.

- **Why do you think Jesus chose a meal as a special way to be with us always?**

Catholics Believe . . .
that Jesus is truly present in Holy Communion.

Catechism, #1374

Body and Blood

At Mass the bread and wine become Jesus' Body and Blood. They still look and taste like bread and wine. But they have become Jesus.

This is a mystery. A **mystery** is something we believe is true, even though we can't explain how it happens.

We call the consecrated bread and wine Holy Communion. **Communion** means being joined together in the closest way. We are joined with Jesus when we receive Holy Communion. Jesus' love becomes a part of us.

Holy Communion joins us to other members of the community, too. Our love for one another grows.

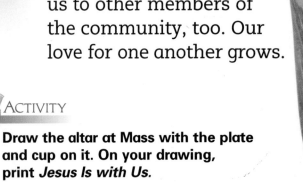

ACTIVITY

Draw the altar at Mass with the plate and cup on it. On your drawing, print *Jesus Is with Us.*

Receiving Holy Communion

When we receive Jesus in Holy Communion, we welcome him with our whole body, mind, and spirit.

Here are steps to follow when you receive Communion:

- Fold your hands and join in singing the Communion hymn as you walk to the altar.

- When it is your turn, you can receive the **host**, or Communion bread, in your hand or on your tongue. When the priest or **Eucharistic minister** says, "The Body of Christ," you answer, "Amen." Step aside, and chew and swallow the host.

- Communion may also be offered from the cup, or **chalice**. After receiving the host, walk to where the cup is offered. The priest or Eucharistic minister says, "The Blood of Christ." You answer, "Amen." Take a small sip.

- Return to your seat, and say a thank-you prayer to Jesus.

Where Will This Lead Me?

Practicing these steps will help you feel comfortable about receiving Holy Communion often.

RECALL

What happens to the bread and wine at Mass?
What do we call something that we believe is true,
even though we can't explain how it happens?

THINK AND SHARE

What is one way you are changed by receiving
Jesus in Holy Communion?

CONTINUE THE JOURNEY

Draw a sign of Holy Communion.

WE LIVE OUR FAITH

At Home Ask family members to tell you
about the first time they received Holy
Communion.

In the Parish Get to know someone
new in your parish community. Remember
that you are all joined with Jesus in the
Eucharist.

Thank You, Jesus!

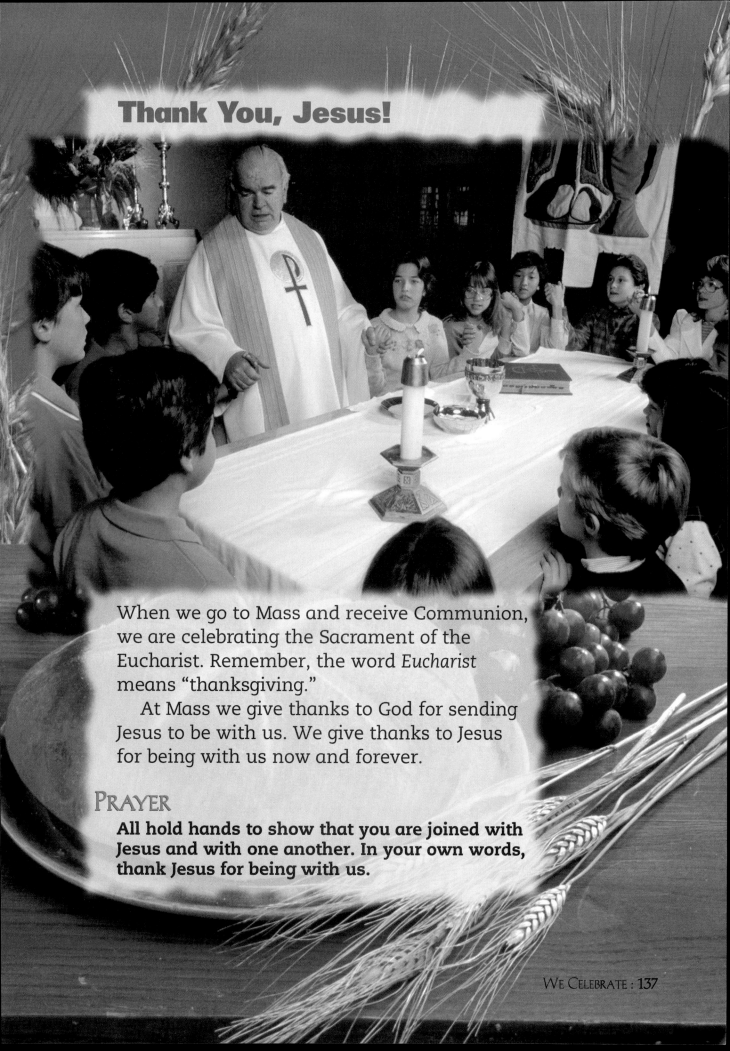

When we go to Mass and receive Communion, we are celebrating the Sacrament of the Eucharist. Remember, the word *Eucharist* means "thanksgiving."

At Mass we give thanks to God for sending Jesus to be with us. We give thanks to Jesus for being with us now and forever.

PRAYER

All hold hands to show that you are joined with Jesus and with one another. In your own words, thank Jesus for being with us.

CHAPTER 23

Members of the Church

PRAYER

Spirit of God, help us be active members of your Church. Help us believe and follow our Lord, Jesus Christ.

"Rich!" his mother called up the stairs, "It's time to go!"

Tonight was a big night for Rich. He was becoming a member of the scouts.

Taking two steps at a time, Rich landed at the bottom of the stairs. He said, "I can't wait until tonight! Club members get to go on field trips and earn patches. They get to have car washes and sell pizzas! They get to . . ."

Rich's dad cut in, "Whoa, buddy! Don't forget the other side of being a member of this club. Remember that you have duties, or *obligations*, too. Next Saturday your club is visiting a care center."

Rich smiled. "I know, Dad. That's one of the best parts of being a scout!"

ACTIVITY

Make up your own club. What would the members of your group do? What obligations would you have?

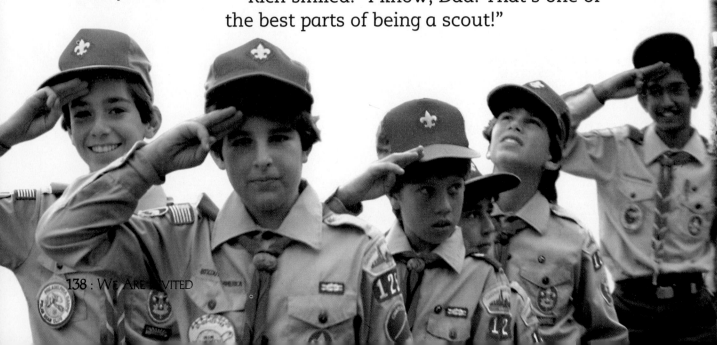

The Duties of the Church

As members of the Church, we, too, have obligations. These duties help us grow in faith and love. Certain duties of Catholics are summed up in the **precepts of the Church**.

We have a duty to worship God together. We go to Mass on Sundays and **holy days**, special days of celebration.

We have a duty to be close to Jesus. We receive Holy Communion at least once a year during the Easter Season. In order to grow in love, we have a duty to turn away from sin. We are required to celebrate the Sacrament of Reconciliation at least once a year when we have committed mortal sin.

We do penance to show that we are sorry for sin. On certain days of the year, Catholics do penance by *fasting* (going without food) or *abstaining* (not eating meat). These acts of penance also bring us closer to our brothers and sisters in God's family who are hungry.

We have a duty to support our Church community. We help the Church by sharing our time, talents, prayers, and money.

ACTIVITY

Read the precepts of the Church on page 179. Draw a picture of yourself carrying out one of these duties.

The sacraments help us celebrate God's grace throughout our lives.

A Sacramental Community

Baptism, Confirmation, and Eucharist make us part of the Church. But our membership does not end there. We celebrate the Sacraments of Baptism and Confirmation only once in our lives, but they mark us for Christ for life. We live them every day. We celebrate our First Communion only once, but we receive the Eucharist as often as possible for the rest of our lives.

The Sacraments of Healing help members of our Church community go through bad times. In Reconciliation we celebrate God's forgiveness and our chance to start over. In the Anointing of the Sick, we trust in God's power to heal our bodies and spirits.

The Sacraments of Service remind us that God wants us to help each other grow in faith. The Sacrament of *Matrimony*, or Marriage, celebrates the love between a man and a woman and the beginning of a new family. The Sacrament of Holy Orders celebrates men who answer God's call to lead and serve the Church. Like Baptism and Confirmation, Holy Orders changes a person for life.

The Spirit Is with Us

Our Church is a sacramental community because the Holy Spirit is with us. The Spirit gives us gifts through the sacraments. These gifts help us grow in faith and love. The **gifts of the Holy Spirit** are listed in this chart:

Scripture Signpost

"Never give up. Eagerly follow the Holy Spirit and serve the Lord."

Romans 12:11

The Gifts of the Spirit

Wisdom	Seeing God's truth
Understanding	Honoring others' feelings
Right judgment or counsel	Making good choices and giving good advice
Courage or fortitude	Standing up for what is right
Knowledge	Learning about God
Reverence or piety	Honoring God with love
Wonder and awe or fear of the Lord	Being open to God's love and power

We can recognize that the Spirit is present by certain signs or qualities. We call these qualities the **fruits of the Spirit**. These qualities include love, patience, kindness, generosity, gentleness, peace, faith, and joy.

- **What signs of the Holy Spirit do you see in your parish community?**

RECALL

Where are certain duties of Church members summed up? What do we call the signs or qualities that tell us the Holy Spirit is present?

THINK AND SHARE

Why are the sacraments such an important part of our lives as Catholics?

CONTINUE THE JOURNEY

Choose one of the gifts of the Holy Spirit. Write a story about someone using this gift.

WE LIVE OUR FAITH

 At Home With your family, make a list of things you can do to make Sunday a real day of rest and prayer.

In the Parish Choose one way to share your time, talent, prayers, or money to support your parish community.

Fill Us with Your Life

The sacraments fill us with the new life of grace. They give us strength to grow in faith. When we celebrate the sacraments, we carry out our duties as Catholics with new energy. We recognize the signs of the Holy Spirit in ourselves and in one another.

Hundreds of years ago new members of the Church sang a song of new life as they prepared to be baptized. It is a song every member of the Church can understand. Pray the words of this song with your class.

PRAYER

1: We come to you, Lord Jesus.

All: Fill us with your life.

2: Make us children of the Father

All: and one in you.

1: The Father's voice calls us,

2: the glory of the Son shines on us,

All: and the love of the Spirit fills us with life.

Review

Which Is Correct? Circle the correct term to complete each sentence.

1. Certain duties of Church members are summed up in the (sacraments, precepts) of the Church.

2. People who stand for the Christian community and agree to help new members are called godparents or (sponsors, Eucharistic ministers).

3. On certain days Catholics do penance by (going to Mass, fasting).

4. Wisdom and courage are two of the (gifts, fruits) of the Holy Spirit.

5. Baptism, Confirmation, and the Eucharist are Sacraments of (Healing, Initiation).

Matching Match the descriptions in Column A with the correct terms in Column B.

Column A	Column B
_____ 1. A kind of Communion bread.	**a.** water
_____ 2. A sign of Baptism.	**b.** chalice
_____ 3. Becoming a member of a community.	**c.** understanding
_____ 4. A cup used at Mass.	**d.** host
_____ 5. The gift of honoring other people's feelings.	**e.** initiation

Share Your Faith A friend asks you why receiving Holy Communion is so important to Catholics. What do you say?

Show How Far You've Come

Use the chart below to show what you've learned. For each chapter, write or draw one important thing you remember.

Jesus Gives Us Sacraments

Chapter 21 The Church Welcomes Us	Chapter 22 Jesus Is with Us	Chapter 23 Members of the Church

What Else Would You Like to Know?

List any questions you have about the sacraments.

_____

_____

_____

Continue the Journey

Choose one or more of the following activities to do. You can do these on your own, with your class, or with your family.

- Look through your Faith Journal pages for Unit Six. Choose your favorite activity, and share it with a friend or family member.

- Write a note to one of the catechumens in your parish. Share your good feelings about the person's being baptized and entering the Church. Pray for the person.

- Make a mural showing how the gifts of the Holy Spirit are present in your parish community.

Good Friday

PRAYER

Jesus, you suffered and died for us. May we never forget your great love.

Holy Week is the week before Easter. During Holy Week we remember the suffering and death of Jesus. On the Friday of Holy Week, called **Good Friday**, we think about Jesus' last hours.

SCRIPTURE STORY
The Road to Calvary

After eating his Last Supper with his friends, Jesus was arrested. He was accused of serious crimes. Even though Jesus was innocent, the Roman governor decided he should be killed.

Soldiers whipped Jesus and made fun of him. They spit at him. They put a crown made of sharp thorns on his head.

Jesus had to carry a heavy wooden cross to the hill called *Calvary*, where he was to die. He was weak, and he stumbled. Soldiers made a man called Simon help Jesus carry the cross.

Most of Jesus' friends had run away when he was arrested. But some of them stayed close by. His mother, Mary, also walked with him to Calvary.

When Jesus reached the hill, the soldiers *crucified* him. They nailed his hands and feet to the cross. They stood the cross up. It was hard for Jesus to breathe.

Two other men were crucified with Jesus. One of them asked Jesus to remember him. Jesus promised this man that he would be welcome in heaven.

Around three o'clock in the afternoon, Jesus lost all his strength. He prayed to his Father. He asked God to forgive those who had made him suffer. He put his life in his Father's hands. Then he died.

A kind man named Joseph offered Jesus' family his own tomb. Jesus' mother and his friends took Jesus' body away to be buried.

—*based on Mark 15:15–47*

Catholics Believe . . .

that Jesus gave his life on the cross for us.

Catechism, #618

Landmark On Good Friday Christians retrace Jesus' last journey in Jerusalem. We call this the *Way of the Cross*. The *stations of the cross* displayed in many churches show moments from Jesus' last hours.

RECALL

Who helped Jesus carry his cross? To whom did Jesus pray on the cross?

THINK AND SHARE

Why do you think followers of Jesus celebrate Good Friday?

CONTINUE THE JOURNEY

Imagine that you meet Jesus on the way to Calvary. What will you say to him? Write your words next to the cross.

_____

_____

_____

_____

_____

_____

_____

_____

_____

_____

WE LIVE OUR FAITH

At Home   With your family, make a cross or crucifix to display in your home. At an evening meal, thank Jesus for his sacrifice.

In the Parish   Look for the stations of the cross in your parish church. Participate in the Good Friday celebration.

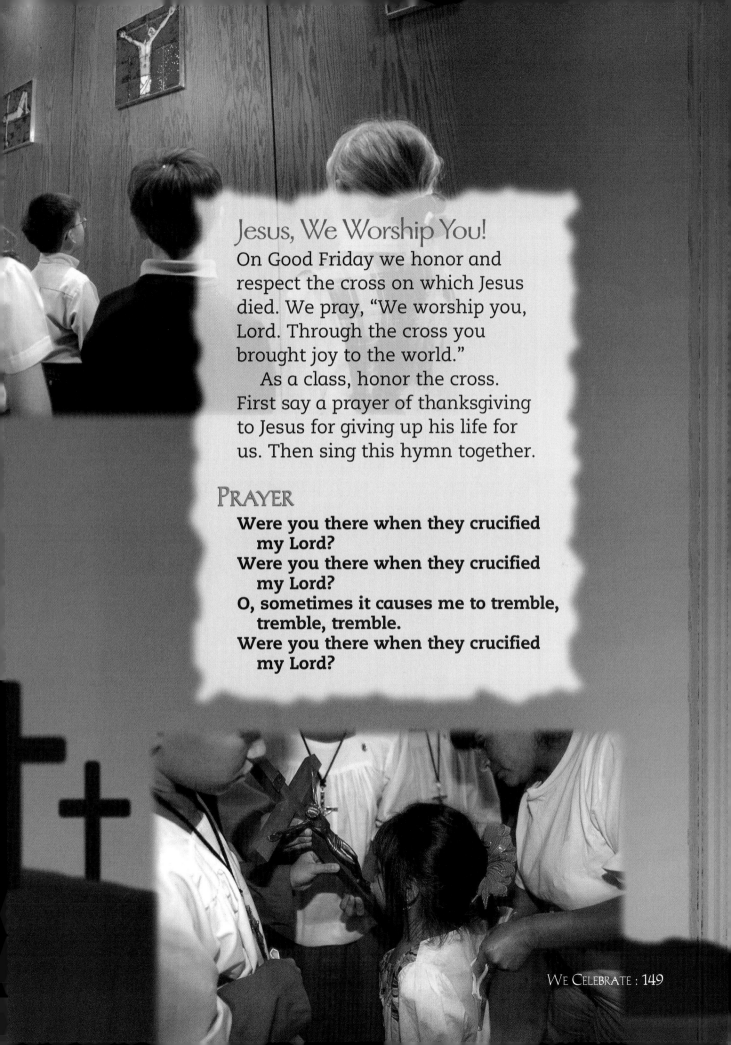

Jesus, We Worship You!

On Good Friday we honor and respect the cross on which Jesus died. We pray, "We worship you, Lord. Through the cross you brought joy to the world."

As a class, honor the cross. First say a prayer of thanksgiving to Jesus for giving up his life for us. Then sing this hymn together.

PRAYER

Were you there when they crucified my Lord?
Were you there when they crucified my Lord?
O, sometimes it causes me to tremble, tremble, tremble.
Were you there when they crucified my Lord?

CHAPTER 25

God Invites Us

PRAYER

You invite us, God, to feast with you forever in heaven. Thank you always for your great kindness!

Have you ever been invited to a wedding *banquet*, or feast? With whom did you go? What did you do? What did you eat?

God invites us to the greatest banquet of all time! He invites us to a sacred banquet where we receive the Eucharist. When we receive the Eucharist, we are filled with God's grace and blessing. We remember God's promise of life with him forever in heaven.

Please Come!

You are invited to a banquet!

When: This Sunday
Where: Your church
Time: During Mass
Given by: God
R.S.V.P.

When God invites us to receive the Eucharist, he is like the man who invited people to a great banquet. Jesus told this story to his followers.

SCRIPTURE STORY

The Great Banquet

A man had prepared a great banquet. He sent his servant to tell his friends that all was ready for the meal to begin. But one guest after another gave an excuse for not coming to the feast.

The man giving the feast was very disappointed. He told his servant to go to every street and alley in town and invite everyone he met. The man said, "I want my home to be full of guests."

—based on Luke 14:15–24

• **Why was the man so disappointed with his friends' response?**

Scripture Signpost

"You treat me to a feast. You honor me as your guest, and you fill my cup until it overflows."

Psalm 23:5

Who invites us to a great feast?

Say Yes to God!

We are like the guests in the Bible story. God invites us to share in a great feast. We can refuse to come. Or we can joyfully accept God's invitation.

God invites us each day to say yes. Here are some ways we say yes to God.

- Obey God's law of love.
- Listen to God's word in the Bible.
- Attend Mass and receive Holy Communion.
- Seek God's forgiveness in the Sacrament of Reconciliation.
- Forgive and love other people.
- Help people in need.
- Pray to God each day.

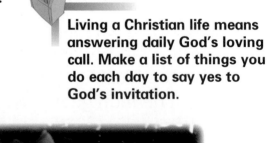

ACTIVITY

Living a Christian life means answering daily God's loving call. Make a list of things you do each day to say yes to God's invitation.

The Eucharist as a Sign

God invites us to share in the great feast of heaven. In heaven our happiness will last forever. We will see God face to face.

In the meantime, we live in God's grace on this earth. God has given us the great gift of the Eucharist. When we celebrate the Eucharist, we have a preview of heaven.

In the Eucharist we receive God's blessings and graces. These are like the blessings and graces we will have forever in heaven.

Every time we receive Holy Communion, we receive the Body and Blood of Jesus. This is the food that makes us live forever in Jesus Christ.

The Eucharist is a sign of what heaven will be like. Receiving the Eucharist helps us look forward to when we will be with God in heaven.

Our Moral Guide

The Eucharist helps us act with love toward others.

Catechism, #1394

How have you acted with love today? In the last week?

Landmark Artists sometimes imagine heaven as a great banquet or feast. The banquet of the Eucharist is like the heavenly feast.

RECALL

What helps us remember God's promise of life forever with him in heaven?

THINK AND SHARE

Why do people sometimes refuse the invitation to be with God?

CONTINUE THE JOURNEY

Write a note to God accepting the invitation to attend his banquet.

WE LIVE OUR FAITH

At Home Look at the list of ways of saying yes to God. Write these on a large poster for the whole family to see.

In the Parish Look around your church at Sunday Mass. Take note of the many people who are there. Pray to God that they all may say yes to God's invitation.

Praise the Lord!

Long before the birth of Jesus, a boy named David was born. He worked as a shepherd and later became a great king.

David wrote many of the **psalms** of the Bible. A psalm is a song of praise to God. Pray this *verse*, or part, of Psalm 23 together.

PRAYER

**Your kindness and love
will always be with me
each day of my life,
and I will live forever
in your house, LORD.**

CHAPTER 26

Jesus Will Come Again

PRAYER

**You promised to be with us always, Jesus.
May we believe in you and have hope.**

Natasha knew that it wouldn't be easy. Some kids have to get used to, or *adjust* to, a new school. But she had to adjust to a new country!

During the summer Natasha had moved with her family from Poland to the United States. She knew she would have to make new friends and go to a new school. She knew she would have to learn to speak a new language.

All this filled Natasha with fear. But she also was filled with hope. She looked forward to her new home in her new country. She hoped to do well in school. She hoped to make new friends.

Fear is natural. But hope is deep within each person.

ACTIVITY

Make up a story about Natasha becoming a member of your class. Include in the story what you would do to make her feel welcome.

The Return of Our Savior

Hope is part of the life of every Christian. At Mass we hear the words, "We wait in joyful hope for the coming of our Savior, Jesus Christ."

Jesus will come to earth again at the end of time. When Jesus returns to earth, he will look at how all people lived on earth. He will judge how well they loved God. He will judge how well they loved other people, especially people in need. This will be **judgment day**.

At that time the **kingdom of God** will come in its fullness. Jesus will reign forever. There will be a new heaven and a new earth filled with people who lived good lives.

Catholics Believe . . .

Christ will return to earth in glory on judgment day.

Catechism, #681

This painting shows one artist's idea of judgment day.

SCRIPTURE STORY
Judgment Day

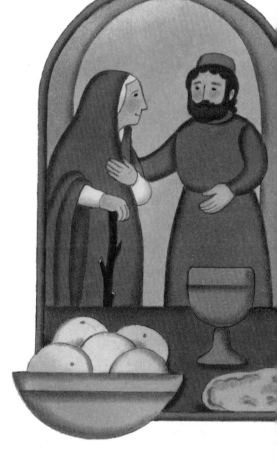

When Jesus returns on judgment day, he will sit on his royal throne. The people of all nations will stand before him. Jesus will separate them into two groups.

Jesus will say to one group, "My father has blessed you! Come and receive the kingdom that was prepared for you before the world was created.

"When I was hungry, you gave me something to eat. When I was thirsty, you gave me something to drink. When I was a stranger, you welcomed me. When I was naked, you gave me clothes to wear. When I was sick, you took care of me."

Then the ones who pleased the Lord will ask, "When did we do these things for you?"

Our Moral Guide

Jesus will judge our actions and our hearts at the end of time. He will ask how we treated the people around us, especially those in need.

Catechism, #678

If you knew Jesus were coming today, how would you act?

Jesus will answer, "Whenever you did these things for any of my people, you did them for me."

On the day of judgment, the people who pleased God will have eternal life.

Jesus will say to the others, "I was hungry, but you gave me nothing to eat. I was thirsty, and you gave me nothing to drink. I was a stranger, but you did not welcome me. When I was naked, you did not give me anything to wear. And when I was sick, you did not care for me.

"Whenever you failed to help any of my people, you failed to help me."

These people will be punished forever. But the ones who pleased God will live forever with God in his kingdom.

—based on Matthew 25:31–46

Saints Walk with Us

Saint Francis de Sales
Feast Day: January 24

Saint Francis de Sales taught people to wait joyfully for when Jesus will come again.

This painting shows Saint Francis de Sales writing a homily.

● Why will Jesus reward those who treat others with justice and charity?

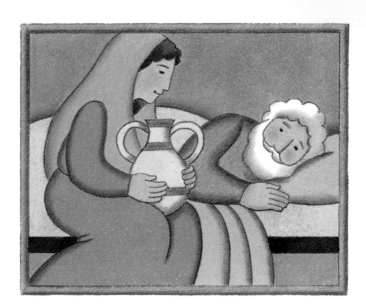

RECALL

What will happen on judgment day? Who will be in the new heaven and the new earth?

THINK AND SHARE

What can we do now to be ready for when Jesus comes again?

CONTINUE THE JOURNEY

Draw a picture of the new heaven and the new earth.

WE LIVE OUR FAITH

 At Home Write down the hopes you have for the future. Write down the hopes you have for your family.

In the Parish Listen to the words of the prayers at Mass. When do we pray for Jesus to come again?

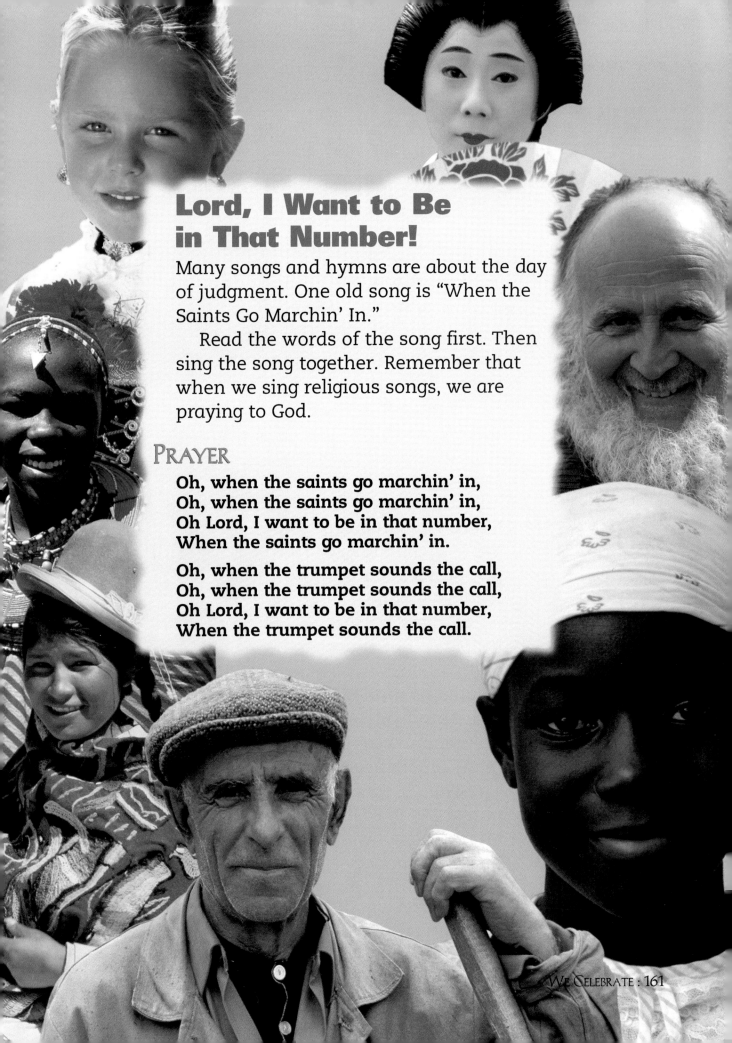

Lord, I Want to Be in That Number!

Many songs and hymns are about the day of judgment. One old song is "When the Saints Go Marchin' In."

Read the words of the song first. Then sing the song together. Remember that when we sing religious songs, we are praying to God.

PRAYER

Oh, when the saints go marchin' in,
Oh, when the saints go marchin' in,
Oh Lord, I want to be in that number,
When the saints go marchin' in.

Oh, when the trumpet sounds the call,
Oh, when the trumpet sounds the call,
Oh Lord, I want to be in that number,
When the trumpet sounds the call.

CHAPTER 27

We Care for the World

PRAYER

Lead us, O God, to work for a more just world. Help us respect all people.

Many children in the world grow up in *poverty*. In a life of poverty, people don't have enough food to eat. They have few clothes. Many have no *shelter*, or place to live.

Jesus has a special love for the poor. As followers of Jesus we try to help people in need. We feed the hungry and give shelter to those who have none.

But there is more to do. People do not choose to be poor or homeless. There are conditions in the world that are *unjust*, or dishonest and unfair. These unjust conditions cause many problems in the world. The Church tries to change unjust conditions. This effort is called working for **social justice**. It is an important work of the Church and all its members.

Landmark The bishops of our Church write letters called *pastoral letters.* These letters often tell Catholics how to work together for social justice and peace.

We Work for Justice and Peace

Every person has certain rights. A *right* is something that is basic to living.

We have the right to life, food, shelter, and clothing. We have the right to a good education. We have the right to be treated with respect.

Often there are forces that refuse people their rights. Sometimes these conditions cause violence.

God asks us to help the Church in its work for justice and peace. Working for justice means making sure people have their rights. It means giving back to people rights that they have lost. Working for peace means creating a world without violence.

How are these children like you? How are they different?

Catholics Believe . . .

that God blesses those who help people who are poor and in need.

Catechism, #2443

Being Peacemakers

Fighting is not the way to solve problems. Jesus asks us to be peacemakers.

Here are steps to follow to be people of peace:

- When you are angry, count to ten. Pray before you act. If necessary, take a time out and walk away.

- Do not call people names. Do not use *harsh*, or hateful, words.

- Talk to the other person to find out the reason the two of you disagree.

- Listen carefully. Try to understand the other person's point of view.

- Tell your point of view. Say what you are feeling and why.

- Work with the other person to find a way to end your disagreement.

- Forgive the other person for any wrong done. Ask forgiveness for any wrong you may have done.

Where Will This Lead Me?

Being able to work out disagreements will help you in all your relationships. You will have more friends. You will be a better team member.

Dorothy Day

Dorothy Day was a Christian who used her life to help the poor and work for justice. In New York she opened *hospitality* houses where people could get food and help. She helped people to see the *dignity*, or worth, of each person.

Dorothy Day was a writer. She started a newspaper called the *Catholic Worker*. She asked people to change unjust conditions that caused problems in the world.

Dorothy Day lived a saintly life. She chose to share the life of people who were poor. She followed Jesus by caring for the poorest of God's children. She gained strength for her work by receiving the Eucharist every day.

Our Moral Guide

Peace is much more than just a world without war. Peace is also a respect for the dignity of every person.

Catechism, #2304

What can you do to show how much you respect everyone in your school?

ACTIVITY

Dorothy Day (above and right center) asked people to live simpler lives. Make a list of three things that mean the most to you. Then ask, "Would I be willing to give one of these up to help others?"

RECALL

What is an example of a right everyone has?

What is social justice?

THINK AND SHARE

Why do disagreements occur between people?

What can be done to prevent them?

CONTINUE THE JOURNEY

Draw a picture of yourself being a peacemaker.

WE LIVE OUR FAITH

 At Home Think of someone who is a peacemaker in your family. Make a card thanking the person for the gift of peace.

In the Parish Find out what people in the parish do to help people who are poor and in need.

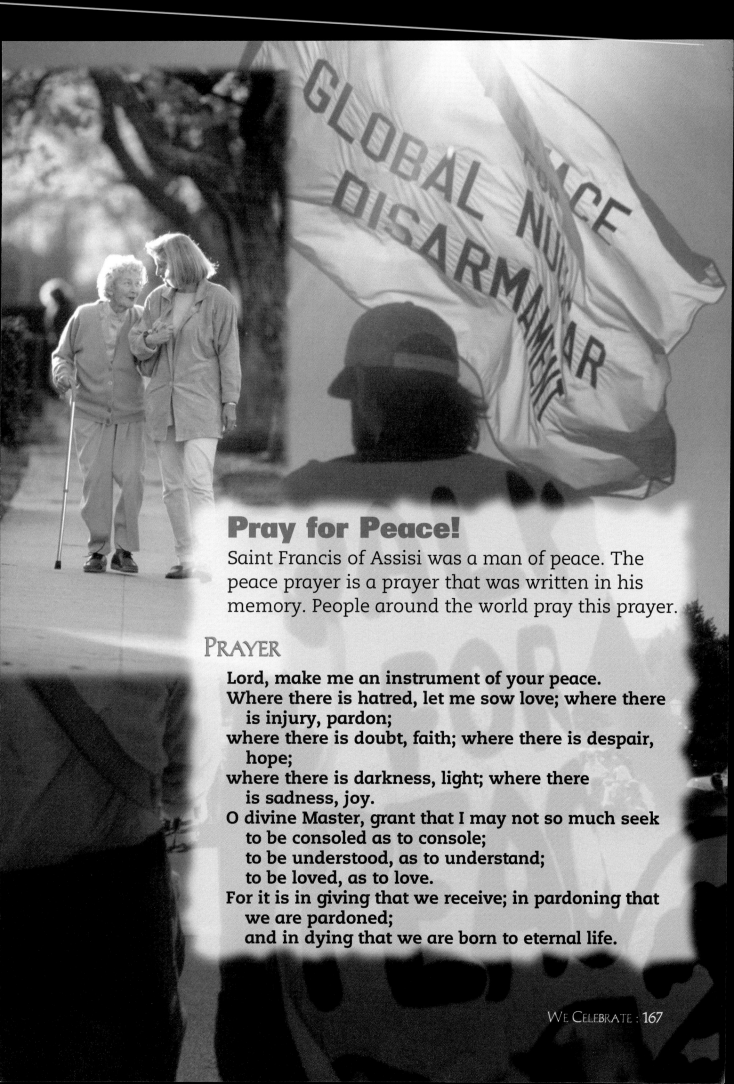

Pray for Peace!

Saint Francis of Assisi was a man of peace. The peace prayer is a prayer that was written in his memory. People around the world pray this prayer.

PRAYER

Lord, make me an instrument of your peace.
Where there is hatred, let me sow love; where there
 is injury, pardon;
where there is doubt, faith; where there is despair,
 hope;
where there is darkness, light; where there
 is sadness, joy.
O divine Master, grant that I may not so much seek
 to be consoled as to console;
 to be understood, as to understand;
 to be loved, as to love.
For it is in giving that we receive; in pardoning that
 we are pardoned;
 and in dying that we are born to eternal life.

Review

Fill in the Blanks
Complete each sentence with the correct term from the word bank.

1. The _____ is a sign of what heaven will be like.

2. On _____ Jesus will judge our lives.

3. Working for _____ means creating a world without violence.

4. The bishops of our Church write _____ letters to tell us how to work for justice.

5. We are called to respect the _____ of others.

Word Bank

judgment day   pastoral   rights   Eucharist   peace

Who Am I?
Match each description in Column A with the correct name from Column B.

Column A

_____ 1. A peace prayer was written in my memory.

_____ 2. I worked for justice.

_____ 3. I taught people to wait joyfully for Jesus to come again.

_____ 4. I wrote psalms.

_____ 5. I will come again.

Column B

a. David

b. Francis of Assisi

c. Francis de Sales

d. Dorothy Day

e. Jesus

Share Your Faith
Someone asks you to explain what Catholics do to help the poor. What do you say?

Show How Far You've Come

Use the chart below to show what you have learned. For each chapter, write or draw one important thing you remember.

Jesus, Lord of All Creation

Chapter 25 God Invites Us	Chapter 26 Jesus Will Come Again	Chapter 27 We Care for the World

What Else Would You Like to Know?

List any questions you have about the Church's work for peace and justice in the world.

_____

_____

_____

Continue the Journey

Choose one or more of the following activities to do. You can do these on your own, with your class, or with your family.

- Look through your Faith Journal pages for Unit Seven. Choose your favorite activity, and share it with a friend or family member.

- Make posters for the parish or school that urge people to work for justice and peace.

- Make up a prayer asking God to help you be a good peacemaker.

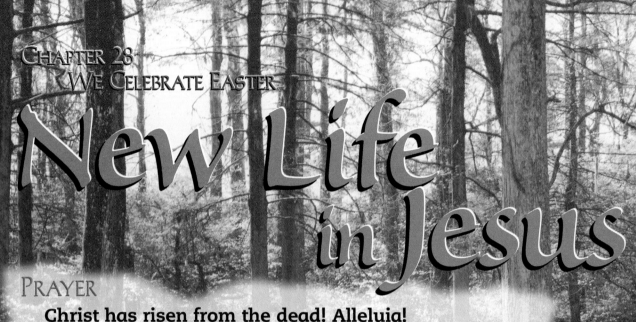

New Life in Jesus

PRAYER

Christ has risen from the dead! Alleluia!
We love you, Jesus!

Jesus died on the cross. His body was taken down from the cross. His body was wrapped in a cloth and buried in a tomb.

What do you think happened next?

SCRIPTURE STORY

The Empty Tomb

Three women who were followers of Jesus went to the tomb very early on Sunday morning. On the way they asked each other, "Who will roll back the huge stone from the entrance?" When they got there, they saw that the stone had already been rolled away.

The women went into the tomb. They saw a young man in a white robe. They were shocked.

The man said, "Don't be alarmed! You are looking for Jesus from Nazareth, who was nailed to the cross. God has raised him to life. He is not here."

The young man continued, "Now go and tell his disciples, and especially Peter, that Jesus will go ahead of you to Galilee. You will see him there, just as he told you."

—based on Mark 16:1–7

Jesus Is Alive

Jesus appeared to various people in the days that followed. He appeared to his apostles. Jesus told them how to carry out his work.

Easter celebrates the **resurrection** of Jesus from the dead. Easter celebrates the new life that Jesus gave us by overcoming death. It is the most important feast in the Church.

Catholics Believe . . .

that because of the resurrection of Jesus, we walk in the newness of life.

Catechism, #654

RECALL

What do we celebrate at Easter? What did the young man say to the women at Jesus' tomb?

THINK AND SHARE

If you were one of the people who found Jesus' empty tomb, what feelings might you have?

CONTINUE THE JOURNEY

Draw a sign that shows the new life of Easter.

WE LIVE OUR FAITH

At Home How does your family celebrate Easter? Talk about why this celebration is so important.

In the Parish Attend Easter services to celebrate the resurrection of Jesus.

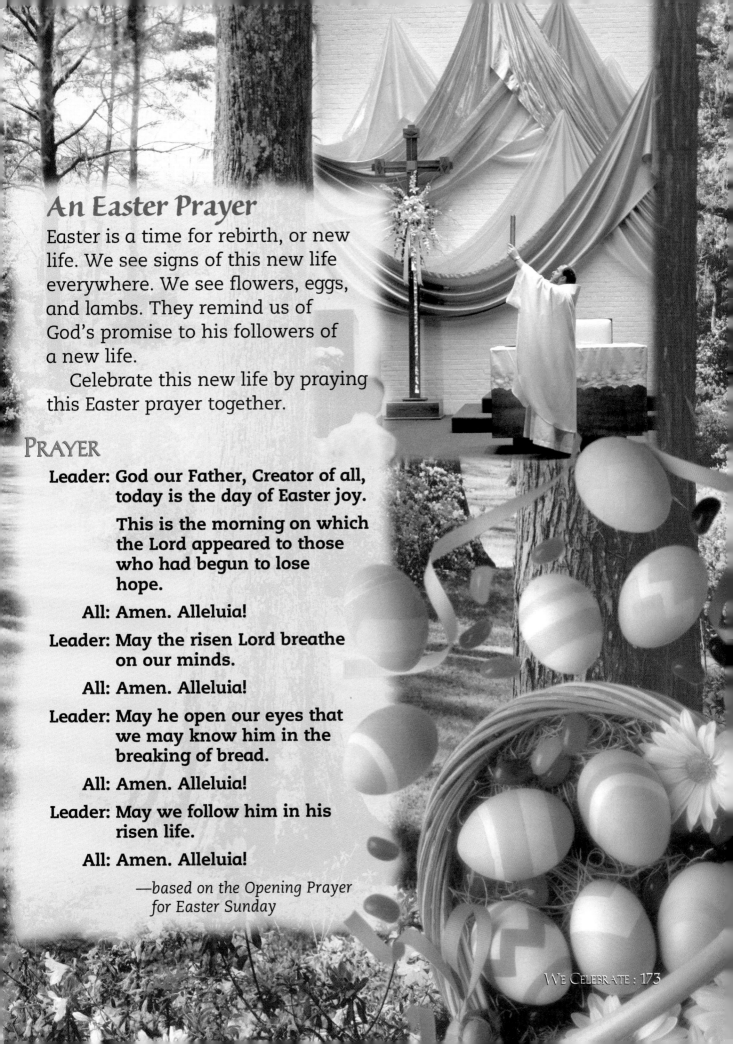

An Easter Prayer

Easter is a time for rebirth, or new life. We see signs of this new life everywhere. We see flowers, eggs, and lambs. They remind us of God's promise to his followers of a new life.

Celebrate this new life by praying this Easter prayer together.

PRAYER

Leader: God our Father, Creator of all, today is the day of Easter joy.

This is the morning on which the Lord appeared to those who had begun to lose hope.

All: Amen. Alleluia!

Leader: May the risen Lord breathe on our minds.

All: Amen. Alleluia!

Leader: May he open our eyes that we may know him in the breaking of bread.

All: Amen. Alleluia!

Leader: May we follow him in his risen life.

All: Amen. Alleluia!

—based on the Opening Prayer for Easter Sunday

CATHOLIC PRAYERS AND RESOURCES

The Sign of the Cross

In the name of the Father, and of the Son, and of the Holy Spirit. Amen.

The Lord's Prayer

Traditional/Liturgical
Our Father,
   who art in heaven,
hallowed be thy name;
thy kingdom come;
thy will be done on earth
   as it is in heaven.
Give us this day our daily bread;
and forgive us our trespasses
as we forgive those who
   trespass against us;
and lead us not into
   temptation,
but deliver us from evil. (Amen)
For the kingdom,
the power, and the glory
   are yours,
now and for ever.

Contemporary
Our Father in heaven,
   hallowed be your name,
   your kingdom come,
   your will be done,
   on earth as in heaven.
Give us today our daily bread.
Forgive us our sins
   as we forgive those who sin
   against us.
Save us from the time of trial
   and deliver us from evil.
For the kingdom, the power,
   and the glory are yours,
   now and for ever.
Amen.

Hail Mary

Hail, Mary, full of grace,
the Lord is with you!
Blessed are you among women,
and blessed is the fruit of your womb, Jesus.
Holy Mary, Mother of God,
pray for us sinners,
now and at the hour of our death.
Amen.

Glory to the Father *(Doxology)*

Glory to the Father, and to the Son, and to the Holy Spirit.
As it was in the beginning, is now, and will be for ever. Amen.

Prayer to the Guardian Angel

Angel sent by God to guide me,
be my light and walk beside me;
be my guardian and protect me;
on the path of life direct me.

Morning Prayer

Almighty God,
you have given us this day.
Strengthen us with your power
and keep us from falling into sin,
so that whatever we say or think or do
may be in your service
and for the sake of your kingdom.
We ask this through Christ our Lord.
Amen.

Evening Prayer

Lord, watch over us this night.
By your strength, may we rise at daybreak
to rejoice in the resurrection of Christ, your Son,
who lives and reigns for ever.
Amen.

Blessing Before Meals

Bless us, O Lord, and these your gifts
which we are about to receive from
 your goodness.
Through Christ our Lord.
Amen.

Thanksgiving After Meals

We give you thanks for all your gifts, almighty God,
living and reigning now and for ever.
Amen.

The Apostles' Creed

I believe in God, the Father almighty,
  creator of heaven and earth.
I believe in Jesus Christ, his only Son, our Lord.
  He was conceived by the power of the Holy Spirit
    and born of the Virgin Mary.
  He suffered under Pontius Pilate,
    was crucified, died, and was buried.
  He descended to the dead.
  On the third day, he rose again.
  He ascended into heaven,
    and is seated at the right hand of the Father.
  He will come again to judge the living and the dead.
I believe in the Holy Spirit,
  the holy catholic Church,
  the communion of saints,
  the forgiveness of sins,
  the resurrection of the body,
  and the life everlasting. Amen.

Act of Faith, Hope, and Love

My God, I believe in you,
I hope in you,
I love you above all things,
with all my mind and heart and strength.

The Jesus Prayer

Lord Jesus Christ,
Son of God,
have mercy on me, a sinner.
Amen.

Act of Contrition

My God, I am sorry for my sins with
  all my heart.
In choosing to do wrong
and failing to do good,
I have sinned against you
whom I should love above all things.
I firmly intend, with your help,
to do penance,
to sin no more,
and to avoid whatever leads me to sin.
Our Savior Jesus Christ
suffered and died for us.
In his name, my God, have mercy.

I Confess

I confess to almighty God,
and to you, my brothers and sisters,
that I have sinned through my own fault
in my thoughts and in my words,
in what I have done,
and in what I have failed to do;
and I ask blessed Mary, ever Virgin,
all the angels and saints,
and you, my brothers and sisters,
to pray for me to the Lord our God.

The Great Commandment

"You shall love the Lord your God with all your heart,
with all your soul, with all your strength, and with all your mind;
and your neighbor as yourself."

—Luke 10:27

The Ten Commandments

1. I am the Lord your God. You shall not have strange gods before me.
2. You shall not take the name of the Lord your God in vain.
3. Remember to keep holy the Lord's day.
4. Honor your father and your mother.
5. You shall not kill.
6. You shall not commit adultery.
7. You shall not steal.
8. You shall not bear false witness against your neighbor.
9. You shall not covet your neighbor's wife.
10. You shall not covet your neighbor's goods.

The Beatitudes

Blessed are the poor in spirit,
  for theirs is the kingdom of heaven.
Blessed are they who mourn,
  for they will be comforted.
Blessed are the meek,
  for they will inherit the land.
Blessed are they who hunger and thirst for righteousness,
  for they will be satisfied.
Blessed are the merciful,
  for they will be shown mercy.
Blessed are the clean of heart,
  for they will see God.
Blessed are the peacemakers,
  for they will be called children of God.
Blessed are they who are persecuted for the sake of righteousness,
  for theirs is the kingdom of heaven.

—Matthew 5:3–10

Precepts of the Church

1. Take part in the Mass on Sundays and holy days. Keep these days holy and avoid unnecessary work.
2. Celebrate the Sacrament of Reconciliation at least once a year if there is serious sin.
3. Receive Holy Communion at least once a year during Easter time.
4. Fast and abstain on days of penance.
5. Give your time, gifts, and money to support the Church.

Works of Mercy

Corporal *(for the body)*

Feed the hungry.
Give drink to the thirsty.
Clothe the naked.
Shelter the homeless.
Visit the sick.
Visit the imprisoned.
Bury the dead.

Spiritual *(for the spirit)*

Warn the sinner.
Teach the ignorant.
Counsel the doubtful.
Comfort the sorrowful.
Bear wrongs patiently.
Forgive injuries.
Pray for the living and the dead.

The Sacraments

Sacraments of Initiation	*Sacraments of Healing*	*Sacraments of Vocation and Service*
Baptism	Reconciliation	Matrimony
Confirmation	Anointing of the Sick	Holy Orders
Eucharist		

Order of the Mass

Introductory Rites

1. Entrance Song
2. Greeting
3. Rite of Blessing and Sprinkling with Holy Water *or* Penitential Rite
4. Glory to God
5. Opening Prayer

Liturgy of the Word

6. First Reading *(usually from the Old Testament)*
7. Responsorial Psalm
8. Second Reading *(from New Testament Letters)*
9. Gospel Acclamation *(Alleluia)*
10. Gospel
11. Homily
12. Profession of Faith *(Creed)*
13. General Intercessions

Liturgy of the Eucharist

14. Offertory Song *(Presentation of the Gifts)*
15. Preparation of the Bread and Wine
16. Invitation to Prayer

17. Prayer over the Gifts
18. Preface
19. Acclamation *(Holy, Holy, Holy Lord)*
20. Eucharistic Prayer with Acclamation
21. Great Amen

Communion Rite

22. Lord's Prayer
23. Sign of Peace
24. Breaking of the Bread
25. Prayers Before Communion
26. Lamb of God
27. Holy Communion
28. Communion Song
29. Silent Reflection or Song of Praise
30. Prayer after Communion

Concluding Rite

31. Greeting
32. Blessing
33. Dismissal

Holy Days

(observed in the United States)

Christmas, the Nativity of the Lord	December 25
Solemnity of Mary the Mother of God	January 1
Ascension of the Lord	40 days after Easter
Assumption	August 15
All Saints' Day	November 1
Immaculate Conception	December 8

Receiving Holy Communion

To receive Holy Communion, you must be free from mortal sin. You must be sorry for any venial sin committed since your last confession. The penitential rite at the beginning of Mass is an opportunity to express your sorrow.

To honor the Lord, we fast for one hour before receiving Holy Communion. Fasting means going without food and drink, except water and medicine.

Catholics are required to receive Holy Communion at least once a year during Easter time. But it is important to receive Holy Communion often—if possible, at every Mass.

Catholics are permitted to receive Holy Communion more than once a day within Mass.

The Sacrament of Reconciliation

Communal Rite of Reconciliation

1. Greeting
2. Reading from Scripture
3. Homily
4. Examination of Conscience *with* Litany of Contrition *and* the Lord's Prayer
5. Individual Confession, Giving of a Penance, and Absolution
6. Closing Prayer

Individual Rite of Reconciliation

1. Welcome
2. Reading from Scripture
3. Confession of Sins and Giving of a Penance
4. Act of Contrition
5. Absolution
6. Closing Prayer

Praying the Rosary

1. Hold the crucifix, and pray the Apostles' Creed.
2. Pray the Lord's Prayer when holding each single bead.
3. Pray the Hail Mary on each bead in a group of three or ten. A group of ten Hail Marys is called a *decade* of the Rosary. Think of one mystery as you pray each decade.
4. After every group of Hail Marys, pray Glory to the Father.
5. Close the Rosary by praying Hail, Holy Queen.

> Hail, holy Queen, mother of mercy,
> hail, our life, our sweetness, and our hope.
> To you we cry, the children of Eve;
> to you we send up our sighs,
> mourning and weeping in this land of exile.
> Turn, then, most gracious advocate,
> your eyes of mercy toward us;
> lead us home at last
> and show us the blessed fruit of your womb, Jesus:
> O clement, O loving, O sweet Virgin Mary.

The Lord's Prayer
Glory to the Father
Hail Mary
Hail Mary
The Lord's Prayer
Glory to the Father
Glory to the Father
Hail Mary
Hail Mary
Hail Mary
The Lord's Prayer
Glory to the Father
Hail Mary
The Lord's Prayer
The Apostles' Creed

Mysteries of the Rosary

Joyful Mysteries	*Sorrowful Mysteries*	*Glorious Mysteries*
1. The Annunciation	1. The Agony in the Garden	1. The Resurrection
2. The Visitation	2. The Scourging	2. The Ascension
3. The Nativity	3. Crowning with Thorns	3. The Coming of the Holy Spirit
4. The Presentation	4. Carrying the Cross	4. The Assumption
5. Finding Jesus in the Temple	5. The Crucifixion	5. The Coronation of Mary as Queen of Heaven

THE LANGUAGE OF FAITH

A

Abba In the language Jesus spoke, a word for "father." Jesus called God by this name.

absolution The forgiveness of sin we receive from God through the Church in the Sacrament of Reconciliation. The word *absolve* means "to wash away."

Advent The Church's four-week season of preparation for Christmas. The word *advent* means "coming."

Advent calendar A way of counting off the days of Advent. Advent calendars usually have a door for each day of the Advent Season. Behind each door is a picture or a Bible verse that helps us prepare for Christmas.

Advent wreath An evergreen wreath in which four candles are set. One candle is lighted for each of the four Sundays of the Advent Season.

altar The table around which we gather to celebrate the Eucharist.

amen A word that means "May it be so" or "Yes!" We say *amen* at the end of a prayer or in response to a statement of belief to show that we agree.

angel A pure spirit created by God, a messenger from God. God gives us each a guardian angel to help us.

Annunciation The holy day we celebrate on March 25. This feast recalls the angel's message to Mary that she was to be the mother of Jesus.

anoint To mark or rub with oil. Anointing is a sign of God's friendship and the presence of the Holy Spirit. It also means healing and strengthening. Anointing is part of the Sacraments of Baptism, Confirmation, Anointing of the Sick, and Holy Orders.

Anointing of the Sick The sacrament that celebrates the healing of body and spirit by Jesus. The Sacrament of Anointing can be celebrated anytime a person is seriously ill or weakened by age.

apostles The twelve special friends and followers of Jesus. The word *apostle* means "one who is sent."

ascension The return of Jesus to his Father after his resurrection. The Feast of the Ascension is one of the holy days.

B

banquet A joyful feast or meal. The Eucharist is a sign of the heavenly banquet we are called to share.

Baptism The first sacrament we celebrate. Baptism makes us children of God and members of the Church, the Body of Christ. It takes away original sin and all personal sin. The word *baptism* means "bath." Baptism is celebrated by pouring water on a person or placing the person in water and praying "I baptize you in the name of the Father, and of the Son, and of the Holy Spirit."

Beatitudes Sayings of Jesus (*Matthew 5:3–10*) that sum up the way to live in God's kingdom and that show us the way to true happiness. The word *beatitude* means "blessedness."

Bible God's word written down by humans. The Bible is the Church's holy book, also called *Scripture*. The Bible is made up of two sections, the Old Testament and the New Testament. There are many different books collected in the Bible. The word *bible* means "library."

bishop A man ordained to lead and teach the followers of Jesus. The bishops are successors of the apostles. A bishop or *archbishop* usually leads a group of parishes called a *diocese* or *archdiocese*. The word *bishop* means "overseer."

blessing Praising God and calling on him to continue to send his gifts. People and things that are blessed are made holy or set aside for God's work.

C

Calvary The place where Jesus died on the cross; a hill outside Jerusalem.

catechumen A person preparing to celebrate the Sacraments of Initiation. The word *catechumen* means "learner."

chalice The wine cup used at Mass.

charity The good habit of showing love for others. Works of charity include sharing what we have with people who are in need and caring for those who are sick or lonely. The word *charity* means "love."

Christ A title for Jesus that means "the anointed one" or "the one chosen by God." Christians take their name from this title. *Christ* is the Greek form of the Hebrew title *Messiah*.

Church The community of Jesus' followers. The Catholic Church is made up of all those who believe in Jesus and is led by the pope and the bishops. A *church* is also the building in which we gather to worship God.

commandment A law of God. The Ten Commandments are laws that tell what God expects of us. The Ten Commandments are summed up in the Great Commandment, which tells us to love God, neighbor, and self.

communion Being joined together in the closest way. In Holy Communion we are joined with Jesus and with one another.

community A group of people who have common beliefs, activities, and goals. A family, a neighborhood, a school, and a parish are all examples of communities.

confess To tell our sins to a priest in the Sacrament of Reconciliation. What we confess to the priest is private.

Confirmation The Sacrament of Initiation that seals and completes Baptism. In Confirmation we are sealed with the Holy Spirit.

conscience The gift from God that helps us know the difference between right and wrong and choose what is right. We must form our conscience properly. We *examine*, or check, our conscience in preparation for the Sacrament of Reconciliation.

consecrate To make holy by the power of the Holy Spirit. At Mass the bread and wine are consecrated. They become the Body and Blood of Jesus Christ.

contrition Sorrow for sin and willingness to do better. Contrition is our first step toward forgiveness. As part of the Sacrament of Reconciliation, we pray a Prayer, or Act, of Contrition.

creation Everything made by God, seen and unseen.

cross A sign of the followers of Jesus. Jesus died on a cross but God raised him to new life, so the cross is a sign of hope. The Sign of the Cross is a prayer we pray while tracing the shape of a cross with our right hand.

crucifix A picture or other image of a cross that shows the body of Jesus. Looking at a crucifix reminds us that Jesus suffered and died for us.

crucify To hang or nail a person to a cross until death. This was a form of the death penalty used by the Roman government in Jesus' time. Jesus was crucified.

custom A special way of doing things, especially sharing meals and celebrating holidays.

D

deacon   A man who is ordained to serve the Church by baptizing, proclaiming the gospel, preaching, witnessing marriages, and doing works of charity.

disciple   A person who follows Jesus and learns from his teachings and actions. The word *disciple* means "one who learns from a master."

Doxology   A prayer of praise to the Holy Trinity.

E

Easter   The Feast of the Resurrection of Jesus Christ, our greatest holy day.

epistles   Another name for the letters written by Paul and other leaders to the early Christian churches. These letters are collected in the New Testament of the Bible. They are read at Mass as part of the Liturgy of the Word.

Eucharist   The sacrament of Jesus' presence under the form of bread and wine. We receive Jesus' own Body and Blood as Holy Communion during the Eucharistic celebration. The Mass is a sacrifice and a holy meal. We join with Jesus to offer him and ourselves to God our Father. The word *Eucharist* means "thanksgiving."

Eucharistic minister   A person specially prepared to assist the priest and other ordained ministers in giving Holy Communion. Eucharistic ministers also carry the Eucharist to parishioners who are hospitalized or unable to attend Mass because of illness or age.

Eucharistic Prayer   The great prayer of thanksgiving prayed by the priest at Mass. During the Eucharistic Prayer the gifts of bread and wine are consecrated by the power of the Holy Spirit. They become the Body and Blood of Jesus Christ.

F

faith   The gift from God that helps us seek him and believe in him.

fasting   Going without food, or eating only a small amount of food, often as an act of penance. We also fast for one hour (taking only water or medicine) before receiving Holy Communion as a sign of respect for Jesus.

Feast of All Saints   November 1, the holy day that celebrates all those who have shown love for God, have followed Jesus, and are now with God in heaven.

free will   God's gift that allows us to choose how to respond to his love for us. Free will is the ability to choose between good and evil. God gave us the gift of free will. God does not force us to do what is right.

fruits of the Spirit   Qualities that show the Holy Spirit is with us. Charity, joy, peace, and patience are some of the fruits of the Spirit.

G

general intercessions   A litany of prayers at Mass in which we ask God to care for the needs of all people.

gifts of the Holy Spirit   Seven gifts given to us by the Holy Spirit in Baptism and Confirmation. These gifts help us grow in holiness.

God   The one, true, divine Being whom we worship. Jesus taught us that God is the Holy Trinity of Father, Son, and Holy Spirit. God created us and loves us.

godparent   A person who agrees to sponsor someone who is baptized. The godparents of a child assist the parents in helping the child grow in the Catholic faith.

Golden Rule   Words of Jesus that tell us how to act. "Treat others as you want them to treat you" (*Matthew 7:12*).

Good Friday   The Friday before Easter. On this day of Holy Week, we remember Jesus' suffering and death on the cross.

gospel   Jesus' teachings about God's love, God's kingdom, and the way we should live. The word *gospel* means "good news." The four books of the New Testament that tell the story of Jesus' life and teachings are called *Gospels*.

grace   God's free, loving gift of himself to us. Grace is God's own life, friendship, and help. We share in God's grace in many ways, especially through the sacraments.

Great Commandment   The teaching that sums up all God's laws. "Love the Lord your God with all your heart, soul, strength, and mind. Love your neighbor as you love yourself" (*Luke 10:27*).

heaven   Life with God forever.

hell   Being separated from God forever. Hell is the result of choosing to live in mortal sin, turning away from God's love and forgiveness.

holiness   Being like God. When we follow Jesus and do what is right, we grow in holiness.

holy   Like God. The word *holy* is also used to describe people and things set apart to serve God in a special way.

Holy Communion   Receiving the Body and Blood of Jesus Christ in the Sacrament of the Eucharist. The word *communion* means "joined closely." In Holy Communion we are joined with Jesus and with one another.

holy day   A special feast day of the Church. We celebrate holy days by participating at Mass and by setting aside time to rest and pray.

Holy Family   Jesus, Mary, and Joseph. Jesus was the Son of God and human like us. He grew up in a human family with Mary, his mother, and Joseph, his foster father.

Holy Orders   The sacrament by which men are ordained to serve God and the Church as deacons, priests, or bishops.

Holy Spirit   The third Person of the Holy Trinity. The Holy Spirit is God's own love and holiness present with us in the Church. Jesus promised that the Holy Spirit would help his followers. The Holy Spirit is one with the Father and the Son.

Holy Trinity   The mystery of one God in three Persons: Father, Son, and Holy Spirit. The word *trinity* means "a unity of three."

holy water   Water that is blessed as a reminder of our Baptism. We make the Sign of the Cross with holy water when we enter or leave a church.

Holy Week   The week before Easter. During these days we recall Jesus' last days among us.

homily   A reflection at Mass given by the priest, deacon, or another minister during the Liturgy of the Word. The homily helps us understand and apply the Scripture readings.

hosanna   A shout of joy that means "Praise God!" When Jesus entered Jerusalem for the last time, people greeted him with shouts of "Hosanna!" and waved palm branches.

hospitality   Making people feel at home. At Mass ministers of hospitality greet parishioners and visitors and welcome them to the Eucharistic celebration.

host   The round, flat wafer of bread that is consecrated at Mass. Small consecrated hosts are used for Holy Communion.

Jesus   A name that means "God saves." This is the name Mary gave to her son, who is the Son of God. We believe that Jesus is both God and human. He taught us about God, his Father. He suffered, died, and was raised from death to save us from the power of sin and everlasting death.

judgment day   When Jesus will return at the end of time to judge all people, living and dead.

K

kingdom of God   God's reign of justice, love, and peace. Jesus came to bring the kingdom of God. It is both here in our midst and yet to come. God's kingdom will come in fullness at the end of time.

L

Last Supper   Jesus' last meal with his friends before he died. At this meal Jesus washed his friends' feet as a sign that they should serve one another. He shared himself with his friends in the form of bread and wine at this meal, which was the first Eucharist.

lay person   A man or woman who has not been ordained. Lay people serve God, the Church, and the world.

Lent   The Church's 40 days of preparation for Easter. We use the time of Lent to grow in love for God and others through prayer, penance, and acts of charity.

litany   A prayer made up of several short petitions or intercessions, with a repeated response after each one. The general intercessions at Mass are in the form of a litany.

liturgy   Our public worship of God in the Mass and the other sacraments.

Lord's Prayer   The prayer Jesus taught his friends, in which we call God "our Father" and pray that God's kingdom will come. The Lord's Prayer is the great prayer of all Christians.

manna   A special food, a little like sweet bread, that God gave to the Israelites as they wandered in the desert. The gift of manna saved God's people from starvation. Manna is a sign of the Eucharist, which saves us from the power of sin and everlasting death.

Mary   The mother of Jesus. God chose Mary to be the mother of his Son. She is the Mother of the Church.

Mass   Our celebration of the Eucharist. At Mass Jesus is present in the community, in the priest, in the word of God, and in Holy Communion.

Matrimony   The sacrament that joins a man and a woman in Christian marriage.

memorial   Anything that helps us remember someone or something important.

memorial acclamation   The statement of faith we pray during the Eucharistic Prayer. The memorial acclamation helps us remember that Jesus died for us, that he was raised from death, and that he will come again in glory.

mercy   God's loving kindness and forgiveness.

Messiah   A Hebrew title that means "the anointed one" or "the one chosen by God." Christians believe that Jesus is the Messiah. *Christ* is the Greek form of this title.

ministry Service to the community that is recognized by the Church. This service honors God. There are many ways lay and ordained persons can minister.

miracle A mighty deed of great power that shows God's love. Jesus' miracles are signs of the kingdom of God.

mission The work the Church is sent to do. The whole Church shares the mission of Jesus, which is to share the good news of God's kingdom. A *mission* can also mean a church built by a missionary.

missionary A person who is sent to bring the good news of God's kingdom to people in other places or distant lands.

moral Having to do with the way we put our beliefs into action. Christian moral life means making choices and acting according to Jesus' law of love, the Beatitudes, the Great Commandment, and the Ten Commandments.

morning offering A prayer asking God to guide all our thoughts, words, and actions of the day.

mortal sin Serious sin. Sin is mortal when it is seriously wrong, when we know that it is seriously wrong, and when we freely do it anyway. Mortal sin breaks our relationship with God and others. The word *mortal* means "deadly."

mystery A truth of our faith that we cannot fully understand, but that we believe because God has shown it to us in Scripture, in the life of Jesus, or in the teaching of the Church. The Holy Trinity is a mystery.

Nativity The Church's name for Christmas, the holy day that celebrates the birth of Jesus. We do not know exactly when Jesus was born, but we celebrate the Feast of the Nativity on December 25.

Nazareth According to the Gospels, the town where Jesus grew up with Mary, his mother, and Joseph, his foster father. Nazareth was in an area called *Galilee* in what is now the country of Israel.

new life Life with God that lasts forever. God raised Jesus from death and gave him new life. If we follow Jesus, we, too, will have new life.

ordained Men who have celebrated the Sacrament of Holy Orders. Deacons, priests, and bishops are ordained ministers. The word *ordained* means "set apart for special work."

original sin The human condition of weakness and tendency toward sin that resulted from the first humans' choice to disobey God.

parable A special kind of teaching story Jesus used to describe the kingdom of God and to tell people how to live in the kingdom. Parables often have surprise endings.

parish A community of Catholics who gather at a particular church for Mass, the sacraments, religious education, and other activities. The leader of a parish is a pastor. Many parishes together make up a diocese or an archdiocese.

Passover The Jewish holy day that celebrates the Israelites' escape from slavery and death in Egypt.

pastor The priest who leads a parish. The word *pastor* means "shepherd." If no priest serves a parish full-time, the parish may be led by an administrator who is a deacon or a lay person.

penance   Prayers or actions we do to make up for our sins. The priest gives us a penance in the Sacrament of Reconciliation. We also do works of penance during Lent to prepare for Easter.

Pentecost   The feast that celebrates the coming of the Holy Spirit to the apostles, 50 days after Jesus' resurrection. The word *Pentecost* means "50 days."

petition   A kind of prayer in which we ask God for what we need. The most common prayers of petition are asking God to forgive our sins or to help us in difficult times.

poverty   Living without enough of the things people need, such as food, clothing, or a home. Justice requires that people who are poor receive what they need. *Spiritual poverty* means depending on God, not material things, for true happiness.

prayer   Many ways of talking to and listening to God. The five reasons for prayer are blessing and adoration, petition, intercession, thanksgiving, and praise.

precepts of the Church   Some of the important responsibilities of Catholics. The word *precept* means "teaching" or "guidance."

priest   A man who is ordained to serve God and the Church by celebrating the sacraments, preaching, and presiding at Mass.

prophet   A person called by God to speak God's message to humans. Every baptized Christian is called to share in the ministry of the prophet.

psalms   Prayers that can be sung. There are 150 of these prayers in the Book of Psalms in the Bible. Jews and Christians use the psalms in prayer and worship. We sing or pray a psalm in response to the first reading at Mass.

R

Reconciliation   The sacrament that celebrates God's forgiveness of sin through the Church. This sacrament is also known as *Penance*. The word *reconciliation* means "coming back together" or "making peace."

religious community   A group of men or women who make promises to serve God and the Church through lives of prayer and action. Members of religious communities are known as religious priests, sisters, nuns, brothers, monks, or friars.

resurrection   The mystery of Jesus being raised from death by God's loving power. We celebrate the Feast of the Resurrection at Easter.

Rosary   A form of prayer to Mary. We pray the Rosary by praying sets of Hail Marys, usually counting off the prayers on a circle of beads. While we pray, we keep in mind important events in the lives of Jesus and his mother. We call these events *mysteries of the Rosary*. The word rosary means "rose garden"; the prayers are like a bouquet we offer to Mary.

S

Sabbath   The Jewish day of rest and worship. The Sabbath begins at sundown on Friday night and lasts until the rising of the first star on Saturday night. In honor of Jesus' resurrection, Christians celebrate Sunday as the day of worship. We celebrate the Eucharist and take time for rest.

sacrament   A sign and source of God's grace. Sacraments are celebrations in which Jesus joins with the community in liturgical actions. Catholics celebrate seven sacraments: Baptism, Confirmation, Eucharist (Sacraments of Initiation); Reconciliation, the Anointing of the Sick (Sacraments of Healing); Matrimony, and Holy Orders (Sacraments of Service). The word *sacrament* means "seal."

sacrifice   To give up something for a greater good. The religious meaning of *sacrifice* is "something precious offered completely to God." Jesus offered himself as a sacrifice on the cross to save us from the power of sin and everlasting death.

saints   People who follow Jesus and show God's love to others. The word *saint* means "holy one." The communion of saints is made up of many kinds of people. We believe that saints are happy forever with God. We celebrate feast days of saints. We ask the saints to pray for us.

Savior   A title for Jesus that means he saved us from the power of sin and everlasting death.

Scripture   Another name for the Bible, the Church's holy book. The word *scripture* means "writing."

sin   The choice to disobey God. Sin can be serious (mortal) or less serious (venial). Sin is a wrong choice made on purpose, not a mistake or an accident. God forgives sin when we are truly sorry.

social justice   Working to make sure that people receive what they need. Social justice sometimes means acting to change unjust laws or attitudes in the community.

Son of God   A title for Jesus that means he is God. The Son is the second Person of the Holy Trinity.

sponsor   A member of the Christian community who is a witness to the promises of an older child or adult celebrating the Sacraments of Initiation.

T

Temple   The central place of worship for the Jews, located in Jerusalem. Outside of Jerusalem Jewish people gathered at houses of prayer and study called *synagogues*. Jesus worshiped and taught at the Temple and in synagogues.

Ten Commandments   A summary of the laws given to the Israelites by God as a sign of the covenant. The first three commandments sum up our duties to God. The next seven commandments sum up our duties to our neighbor.

V

venial sin   Less serious sin. Venial sin weakens, but does not destroy, our friendship with God. Continuing to do what is wrong in less serious matters can lead to choosing what is wrong in more serious matters.

virtue   A good quality or habit of goodness.

vow   A sacred promise. Christians make vows in the Sacraments of Baptism, Holy Orders, and Matrimony. Members of religious communities also make vows.

W

Way of the Cross   A way of remembering, in prayers and actions, Jesus' suffering and death. Pictures, statues, or crosses that show or mark the events of Jesus' suffering and death are called *stations of the cross*. We pray the Way of the Cross during Lent, especially during Holy Week.

works of mercy   Actions that show justice, love, and peace, as Jesus did. The Church's list of actions that care for people's physical needs are called *Corporal Works of Mercy*. Actions that care for people's spiritual needs are called *Spiritual Works of Mercy*.

worship   Praising and honoring God in prayer and liturgy.

INDEX

A

Abba, 31
absolution, **116**
abstaining, **139**
Act of Contrition, 177
Act of Faith, Hope, and Love, 176
Advent, **74**–77
African prayer, 35
All Saints' Day, 50–53
Andrew, Saint, 55
angels, **26**, 99
Annunciation, **29**
anoint, **129**
Anointing of the Sick, Sacrament of, 38, 140
Apostles' Creed, 176, 182
Ash Wednesday, 122–123
asking prayer, 45

B

Baptism, Sacrament of, **37**–38, 40
    as first sacrament, 126–131, 140
    reminder of, 22, 41
Basil, Saint, 140
Beatitudes, **104**, 111, 178
Bethlehem, 7, 74, 98–99
Bible, **15**–17
    first people in, 19
    psalms of, 155
    readings during Mass, 92
    See also Scripture
bishop, 38, 86
blessing, 63, 153
Blessing Before Meals, 65, 175
Blood of Christ, 91, 133–135, 153
Body of Christ, 91, 127, 133–135, 153
bread, 14, 60–65, 135

C

Calvary, 146–148
catechumens, **127**
celebration
    Advent, 74–77
    Easter, 170–173
    of Eucharist, 93
    of forgiveness, 114–119
    of holy days, 139
    of Holy Spirit, 47
    Lenten, 122–125
    Passover, 61
    sacraments as, 37–38
chalice, **135**
charity, **122**
choices, 116
    making, 55, 108–113
    moral, **109**–113
Christ, **21**   See also Jesus
Christians, early, 39, 80, 105
Christmas
    carol, 101
    celebrating, 98–101
    getting ready for, 74–77
Church, **79**, 84
    becoming member of, 38
    caring for world, 162–167
    as community, 78–83, 92, 139
    leaders of, 81, 86

members of, 128, 138–143
    mission of, 85–88
    precepts of, **139**, 179
    remembering Jesus, 90–95
    teachings of, 111
    welcoming us, 126–131
commandment   See Great
    Commandment; Ten
    Commandments
communion, **134**   See also Eucharist,
    Sacrament of; Holy Communion
community, **78**
    Church as, 78–83, 92, 139
    early Christian, 39
    laws in, 103
    religious, 86
    sacramental, 140–143
confession   See Reconciliation,
    Sacrament of
Confirmation, Sacrament of, 38,
    127–128, 140
conscience, **110**, 117
consecrate, **133**
contrition, **115**, 119, 177
creation, 6–11, **14**, 17, 37
cross, 22, 56
    Jesus' death on, 21, 56, 170
crucifix, 21
crucifixion, 147
customs, **123**

D

David, 155
Day, Dorothy, 165
deacon, 37–38, **86**
death, 21, 38, 171
dignity, **165**
disciples, **56**
Doxology, 174

E

Easter, 131, 139, 170–173
    forty days before, 122
    week before, 146
Easter Prayer, 173
Elizabeth, Saint, 53
Elizabeth of Hungary, Saint, 63
epistles, **39**
Eucharist, Sacrament of, 38, **91**–95,
    137, 140
    as God's invitation, 150–155
    Jesus in, 74, 133–136
    as Sacrament of Initiation, 127–128,
    140
    See also Holy Communion; Mass
Eucharistic minister, **135**
Eucharistic Prayer, 95
Evening Prayer, 175
examination of conscience, 117

F

faith, 95, 141
family
    Holy, **8**–10, 13, 98–99
    praying with, 34, 64, 87
fasting, **139**

Father
    God as, 30–35, 42, 44, 59
    See also God, Holy Trinity
Feast of All Saints, **53**
Feast of the Annunciation, 29
Feast of the Holy Trinity, 47
Feast of the Nativity, 98, 100
First Communion, 140   See also
    Eucharist, Sacrament of;
    Holy Communion
forgiveness
    celebrating, 114–119
    God's, 38, 110
    Jesus', 66–71
Francis of Assisi, Saint, 167
Franciscan Peace Prayer, 167
Francis de Sales, Saint, 159
free will, 108
fruits of the Spirit, **141**

G

Gabriel, Angel, 26, 29
general intercessions, **89**
gifts of the Holy Spirit, **141**
Glory to the Father, 174, 182
God, 8, 15
    as Creator, 19
    forgiveness of, 67, 110, 114
    inviting us, 150–155
    kingdom of, 85, **157**
    life from, 36–41
    love of, 12–23, 36, 63
    praising, 17, 107
    saying yes to, 26–29
godparent, 40, **128**, 130–131
Golden Rule, **103**
Good Friday, **146**–149
Gospel stories, 71
grace, **37**–40, 42, 127
    life of, 126, 131, 143
Great Commandment, **104**–106, 111,
    178

H

Hail Mary, 27, 29, 174, 182
Healing, Sacraments of, 38, 140
heaven, **31**, 153
Hildegard of Bingen, 13
holiness, **51**–52
holy, **8**
Holy Communion, 92–93, 134–136,
    139, 181   See also Eucharist,
    Sacrament of
holy days, **139**
Holy Family, **8**–10, 13, 98–99
Holy Orders, Sacrament of, 38, 86, 140
Holy Spirit, 38, 42–47, 127
    gifts of the, 141
    as helper, 57, 111, 113, 117–118
    See also God, Holy Trinity
Holy Trinity, **44**, 47   See also Father,
    God, Holy Spirit, Jesus Christ
holy water, 22, 41, 125
Holy Week, **146**
homily, 93
hosanna, **17**
host, **135**

Boldfaced numbers refer to pages on which the terms are defined.

I

I Confess, 177
Initiation, Sacraments of, 38, **127**–131, 140
Islamic prayer, 35

J

Jesus, 15, **21**, 37, 43, 51
    birth of, 7, 74, 98–101
    Body and Blood of, 91, 133–135, 153
    as Bread of Life, 60–65
    Church remembers, 90–95
    death of, 146–147, 170
    following, 56, 79–80, 84–89
    forgiveness from, 66–71
    God as Father of, 30–35
    inviting us to love, 102–107
    as Light of the World, 77
    lessons about God from, 42, 44
    love of, 13–14, 54–59, 162
    new life in, 170–173
    resurrection of, 170–173
    sacrifice of, 56, 91, 94
    as Savior, **21**–22
    second coming of, 156–161
    stories of, 14, 68
    See also Son of God
Jesus Prayer, 23, 177
Jewish people, 61
Jewish prayer, 35
John, Saint, 43, 105
John the Baptist, Saint, 75
John Vianney, Saint, 81
Joseph, Saint, 7–9, 13, 53, 98–99
Judaism *See* Jewish people
judgment day, **157**–161
justice, 162–163

K

kingdom of God, 85, **157**

L

Last Supper, 91, 133, 146
laws, 103, 107, 111
lay people, 86, 88
leaders, Church, 81, 83
Lent, **122**–125
litany, 119
liturgy, 180 *See also* Eucharist; Mass
Lord, 21 *See also* Jesus
Lord's Prayer, **33**–34, 174, 182
love
    God's, 12–23, 36, 43, 63, 134
    Jesus and, 43, 54–59, 102–107
    as one of the fruits of the Spirit, 141
    parish as community of, 79

M

manna, **63**
marriage, 38, 86, 140
Mary, Mother of God, 7–9, 13–14, 23, 26–29, 98–99, 147
Mass, 17, 59, 79, 87, 92–93, 136, 180
    Eucharist during, 95, 133
    lay ministers at, 86
    Scripture readings at, 15–16, 39

Matrimony, Sacrament of, 38, 86, 140
Maximilian Kolbe, Saint, 104
meal prayers, 65, 175
memorial acclamation, 95
mercy, 23, **67**–70
    prayer for God's, 71
    works of, 179
Messiah, 21 *See also* Jesus; Son of God
ministry, **86**
miracle, **63**–64
mission, **85**
missionaries, **85**, 87
morality, 8, 32, 39, 55, 92, 105, 111, 128, 134, 158, 165
morning offering, 59
Morning Prayer, 175
mortal, **110**
mortal sin, **110**, 116, 139, 181
Mysteries of the Rosary, 182
mystery, 95, **134**

N

Native American prayer, 35
Nativity, Feast of the, **98**, 100
Nazareth, 13
new life, 22, 129, 143, 170–173

O

oil, 14, 21, 115, 129
ordained, 86
Our Father *See* Lord's Prayer

P

parables, **68**
parents, 60, 87, 131
parish, **79**, 87, 100
Passover, 61
pastor, **81** *See also* priest
pastoral letters, 163
Paul, Saint, 39
peace, **101**, 141, 163–165
Peace Prayer, 167
penance, **116**, 118 *See also* Reconciliation, Sacrament of
penitential rite, 70, 112
Pentecost, **47**
Peter, Saint, 43, 53 *See also* Simon
petition, **45**
prayer, 32, 71, 80, 83, 113, 122, 161
    See also titles of individual prayers
Prayer to the Guardian Angel, 174
precepts of the Church, **139**, 179
priest, 37, 81, 116, 133, 135
    Holy Orders for, 38, 86
promise, 18–23, 43, 77, 131
prophet, **75**
psalms, **155**

R

Reconciliation, Sacrament of, 38, 114–119, 139–140, 181
relationship, 31, 37, 67, 164
religious sisters and brothers, 86
religious songs, 161
rite, **41**
    penitential, 70, 112
    of Reconciliation, 116
rosary, 182

S

Sabbath, **61**
sacramental, 123
sacramental community, 140–143
sacraments, **37**–38, 179 *See also individual sacraments*
Sacraments of Healing, 38, 140
Sacraments of Initiation, **127**–131, 140
Sacraments of Service, 38, 140
sacrifice, **55**–59
    Jesus', 56, 91, 94
    Lent as time of, 122–125
sadness, 19, 21, 118, 122
saints, **50**–53 *See also individual names of saints*
Savior, **21**–22, 157–161
Scripture, **15**–16, 133
    readings during Mass, 86, 93
    See also Bible
second coming of Jesus, 156–161
Service, Sacraments of, 38, 140
Sign of the Cross, 22, 44, 125, 174
signs, 12–17, 43, 153
Simon, 55–56, 115 *See also* Peter, Saint
sin, **19**, 21–23, 116, 122, 181
    choice and, 109–110
    forgiveness for, 66, 114–119
    turning away from, 131, 139
social justice, **162**
Son of God, 7–11, 19, 37, 44, 98–99, 114 *See also* Jesus
songs, religious, 161
sponsor, **128**, 130
stations of the cross, 147–148
stories, 14–15, 68

T

Ten Commandments, **103**, 107, 111, 178
Thanksgiving After Meals, 65, 175

V

venial, **110**, 116, 181
vows, **131**

W

water, 14, 22
    baptismal, 41, 129
Way of the Cross, 147
Works of Mercy, 179
world, 12–17
    beginnings of, 6–11
    caring for, 162–167
worship, 79, **80**